Critical Praise for *Random* by Penn Jillette

"*Random* is everything you would hope from Penn Jillette and so much more. Random numbers are seemingly crazy, unconnected, and unpredictable: this fabulous, wondrously compelling, funny, and original novel is all that too. As for laughs—it passed the fling-up-the-head-snort-and-slap-the-thigh test a dozen times in the first few pages alone. Hugely recommended."

—Stephen Fry, actor/writer

"Jillette's latest novel, *Random*, is about a young man who inherits his father's crushing debt to a loan shark and turns to dice—and other dangerous measures—to dig himself out. That the dice bring him luck sends him a new philosophy of leaving decisions both big and small up to chance." —*New York Times*

"Jillette (*Presto!*), the magician best known as the verbal half of Penn and Teller, unveils an entertaining Las Vegas picaresque . . . Jillette's acerbic wit and perfect pacing keep this afloat. Readers will hope Jillette has more fiction up his sleeves." —*Publishers Weekly*

"Jillette is one of our weirder national treasures . . . [His] unironic hero is Bobby Ingersoll, a nobody who makes his living driving strip club ads up and down the Strip . . . After accidentally ripping off some gangbangers during a botched robbery, Bobby drops it all on a roll of the dice and suddenly finds himself a multimillionaire with an epiphany: 'The Dice now owned Bobby. He owed his life to Chance' . . . An average joe's free-spirited, madcap romp through the last days of American empire." —*Kirkus Reviews*

"Penn Jillette is half of Penn & Teller, the longest-running magic show in Las Vegas. This is his crime-fiction debut, and he has put together a wild story set in Sin City that is sinfully diverting . . . [A] crackerjack caper." —*Booklist*

"*Random* is a corker about a Vegas guy in a tight spot who has a stroke of luck—and turns it into a life philosophy. It hits the world on Oct. 11—place a bet on it." —*CultureWag*

"Bravo, Bobby Ingersoll. Encore, Penn Jillette!" —Debbie Harry

"The reader on your list who loves to laugh will thoroughly enjoy *Random* by Penn Jillette. It's the story of an almost-twenty-one-year-old who inherits a pile of debt from his horrible father, and it's due to the (even more horrible) loan shark when the guy turns twenty-one. Will a roll of the dice eliminate all his problems? Lucky is the person who gets this book, to find out." —*QSaltLake Magazine*

"As conjured up by Penn Jillette, master magician and best-selling author of both fiction and nonfiction, *Random* takes us on a crazy, dizzy, and inventive journey in which Las Vegas born and bred Bobby Ingersoll opts to let Chance guide his life . . . Like a night in Vegas experienced with a buzz on, this all becomes a tipsy ride . . . Entertaining reading for anyone who likes a gamble." —*Mystery Scene*

"[*Random*] is the story of Bobby Ingersoll, who finds himself responsible for his father's gambling debts, and who places his faith—or something like it—in 'Random,' the philosophy of basing life choices entirely on the roll of his 'lucky' pair of dice. What follows is a rollicking exploration of what happens when we give over every decision—from what to eat to whom to marry to how or when to die—to the random fall of two numbered cubes." —*Tulsa World*

"The book explored an interesting story that could have gone very differently if someone actually tried to live by the dice in this manner, but then again, if Bobby's life had immediately crashed and burned, it would not have made for a very interesting novel." —*Game Vortex*

"In *Random*, Jillette taps into material from his own life as a wise-ass magician/smartest-guy-in-the-room/very public atheist/skeptic and throws one of his magician pals Piff the Magic Dragon into the expository, humorous mix . . . [U]ltimately, [Penn]'s a convincing sonofabitch and a wily tale-teller and you're happy to go along for the ride." —*Book and Film Globe*

FELONY JUGGLER

by

Penn Jillette

BROOKLYN, NEW YORK

Published by Akashic Books
©2025 Penn Jillette

ISBN: 978-1-63614-238-8
Library of Congress Control Number: 2024949339

Akashic Books
Brooklyn, New York
Instagram, X, Facebook: AkashicBooks
info@akashicbooks.com
www.akashicbooks.com

As always for:
Emily
Mox
Zolten

CHAPTER 1

There were two things I wanted in high school: I wanted to be Jewish. I wanted to be gay. I listened to Lenny Bruce, and he talked about the goyim and that was me. In *Do the Right Thing* Spike Lee says to John Savage, with disdain, "Go back to Massachusetts." I wasn't from smart Massachusetts, like Cambridge. I wasn't even from dumb tough Massachusetts like Dorchester or Revere. I was from the part of Massachusetts that doesn't matter to anyone. The Massachusetts that no one even thinks about. People kind of know the Western Mass of Tanglewood, Amherst, the Five Colleges, the Arlo Guthrie stuff, but they didn't even know Greenfield, Massachusetts existed until Anthony Bourdain talked about the opioid capital of New England, and that was decades later. It's now the fentanyl capital of New England, but back when I was a teenager, it wasn't even that.

As the 1970s started, Greenfield was a combination of hippie and redneck, like a lot of America. There were flannel shirts and gun racks, hunting, fishing, and the Brotherhood of the Spirit huge hippie commune, with rich kids like Walter Cronkite's daughter giving money to a spiritual, sexy ex-con— Michael "Rapunzel" Metelica.

School was awful. All the acid heads getting teaching degrees at the University of Massachusetts would try out their "open campus," "free school" theoretical techniques in our dead factory town, so our Greenfield High was experimental nothing. No real classes, no nothing. Even more of a waste of time than every other high school.

I had good SATs. Crazy good. I had a free ride to any college, but I didn't want to go. I give a different reason every time I'm asked. I had never done drugs or had a drink and college seemed like just drugs and alcohol and I didn't want it. I was already getting laid, so I didn't need it. I skipped most all my classes in my senior year of high school to drive the million miles to Amherst in twenty-five minutes and sat in on classes there. I was six foot seven, with hair down the middle of my back—certainly college material, but it didn't seem like college was hard enough or interesting enough. Of course, if I'd had MIT or Harvard to kick my ass, it might have been different, but things are never different, things are what they are.

I was a Greenfield goy and there was no way out of it. I was big, dumb, full of cum, with a little nose, and I liked pussy. Dull. I read *Steal This Book*, *Revo-*

lution for the Hell of It, Woodstock Nation, and the *East Village Other.* I memorized Lenny Bruce. I listened to Bette Midler and thought a lot about sucking cock, but mostly as an intellectual exercise. I was really fucking lots in high school and very happy with that, but it was all women. Anal sex was birth control, and the anal sex was with women. I was smart enough to fuck smart girls, so Henry Miller did all the hard seduction work and I just showed up with a cock, a rebellious attitude, and long hair, and I was in.

I wasn't even out of school when I took my first long hitchhiking trip. It was around March, around spring break. My best friend in high school, Larburg, was a year older and he'd graduated from Greenfield High and moved to Chicago to go to college. Rather, he moved to Antioch to go to college in Ohio, but Antioch was such a hippie college that you didn't even go there, you went there and then they sent you on a work/study to Chicago. I don't know how the fuck college works.

I decided to hitch out to Chicago to visit Larburg. I convinced my high school juggling partner, Adam, to come with me. That wasn't hard. I still don't know how we got our parents to go for it. No idea. I don't even remember having to try. We took a trip up to L.L.Bean in Maine and bought good backpacks. I got a passport so I'd have good ID for the police. I sewed a hundred bucks into the lining of my backpack. That hundred bucks might still be there in the probably rotted knapsack in the attic above the garage, along with the notarized note from my mom and dad stating that I wasn't a runaway. Mom and Dad drove us to the rotary at Route 91 and the Mohawk Trail, right at the Howard Johnson's where I'd washed dishes. By the time they'd swung around the other side of the restaurant, we'd gotten our first ride, and we were off to Chicago. How did they let us do that? Times were different. We know that statistically things were more dangerous back then, but they seemed safer, maybe because there was less news. Maybe because there were fewer movies made at that time. I don't know. No one hitchhikes anymore, but hitchhiking is so healthy. You meet people and you save gas. But we're all more scared of each other now than we were then. People hated hippies, though they didn't mind letting them into their cars for a while.

There was no GPS. Instead, we had maps that our parents got from the American Automobile Association, but we couldn't read them. People say that GPS has ruined people's ability to read maps and navigate. Maybe it did that for *you*. But for me, until GPS came along I never knew where I was. I never learned to read a map. It wasn't a proper subject in high school. Neither was balancing a checkbook, for that matter. How hard could it be to get to Chicago? It was the next city over, right? If we were going somewhere, and it wasn't to Boston, we had to be going to Chicago— it's just the other way. Like Montreal. The first couple rides took us to Montreal. It seemed on the way. Chicago was cold, Montreal was cold, who cares?

By evening, late evening of the first day of hitching, we were in Montreal. We'd gotten rides from college students leaving UMass for spring break. These students were too stupid to go to Florida. We had all just been declared 1-H in the draft. We were essentially on hold, and with war, hold is a good place to be. Vietnam wasn't going to draft us, so getting into Canada was not an issue. We crossed the border without incident.

There we were, somewhere in Montreal. Adam and I were at some interchange. It was outside a toll booth or something. The police wouldn't let us near anywhere warm. We were singing Paul Simon, "*Detroit, Detroit, got a hell of a hockey team*," repeatedly and we were freezing. We were going to freeze to death. That's where the story could have ended, leaving no one left to tell the tale. It was cold. Militarized cold. If you're in Massachusetts, why do you hitchhike north? Why would a couple fellows do that?

I remember distinctly that we couldn't get a ride out of Montreal because someone had picked up a couple hitchhikers in Montreal just the night before and those hitchhikers had raped and murdered them. We were hitchhiking in Montreal, and a hitchhiking murderer and rapist was all over the news. That's why we weren't getting picked up. I remember it so clearly that it must not have been true. How would we have known that? We didn't have a radio. We didn't buy a newspaper. Would someone have stopped to tell us that? Who pulls over to say, "Hey, someone like you raped and killed someone so no one is going to pick you up, sorry"? We must have made that up.

It was drizzling. It was so fucking cold. There

was still snow and slush all over. It was not Florida spring break, that's for sure. It was a wet T-shirt contest all right, but no one was cheering, and the prize was staying alive. You like my nipples rock hard? Well, you should have been there. I had on my yellow work boots with little psychedelic paisleys that my girlfriend had painted all over them, and they were covered with salt and slush and soaking through the waterproofing. The hems of my yellow elephant bell-bottoms were frozen stiff like the Liberty Bell, crack and all. The parts of my hair that weren't frozen were pushed down under my hat, trying for insulation.

"Someone has to pick us up, right?" Adam forced out between frozen, clenched teeth.

"Why? Why? If one person can go by, another can go by. If one person doesn't have to pick us up, no one has to. If you flip a coin a million times heads, it can come up heads again. At that point maybe it's two-headed. Maybe the next car that comes by has the same reason not to pick us up as the last car." Maybe that's when we made up the rapist story and then believed it.

Across a snowy field, there was a slow train. A really slow train, just barely moving. The snow was about a foot deep and there was a fence, but we could get to the train.

"Let's go hop that train," I said.

"Do you know how to hop a train?"

"I think you just jump onto it, right? I mean, you *hop* on."

"We don't know how."

"If we stay here, we freeze to death. The train at least gets us out of here. We freeze to death somewhere else."

Running across a field with a backpack and frozen feet is not easy, but we were not the first teenagers to do it, and no one was shooting at us. We got over the barbed wire, with a few small cuts on our hands and legs, and ran. Suddenly we were close to the train. Now, a slow-moving train is still a moving train, and slow moving for a train is not slow moving even when you're sprinting next to it. We could keep up with it, but not for long. So, while running alongside the train, I reached out for the ladder between two cars. I was wearing gloves, but they were soaked through, partially frozen, and there was blood inside from the barbed wire cuts. I pulled my jacket down over my hands and lunged for the ladder. It almost pulled my arms out of their sockets. The train did not slow down with my weight. I was a tick on a deer's ass. Adam was still running beside the train.

"Get on, asshole! Grab on, just grab on!" I was screaming.

"Let go, get off!" I could just barely hear him, the sound eaten up by the speed, the cold, and the dark.

"No, join me! Jump on—now!" Really screaming. I didn't want to be leaving Montreal alone. I also didn't want to leave Montreal with Adam. I didn't want to be in Montreal alone. I didn't want to be in Montreal with Adam. I wanted to be somewhere warm and dry, with or without Adam. Who cares?

Adam finally hopped on, but a bunch of cars behind me. Neither one of us was really on the train. We were both holding on by our hands with our legs dangling behind us, trying to get them on the ladder. We finally did that. Now what?

The train sped up as we held desperately onto freezing ladders, moving into the dark, going faster and faster. It was now a speeding train, away from the intersection lights of Montreal in no time. It was dark, just train lights and houses in the distance. I couldn't even really see Adam. There was enough wind that it would have been impossible to talk anyway. All we could do was hold onto freezing, speeding ladders that we couldn't see. I was so tired and cold and wet. If I didn't move, I'd just hang there until I froze or fell asleep, or dropped into the snow and died. Just a piss-hole in a Canadian snowbank. This had gone from a tender goodbye from Mom and Dad at the Mohawk Trail rotary to disaster in under twelve hours.

I decided I had to get to Adam. I can't remember how I did it. I don't think it was possible to walk between the cars. It was all freight, there were no passengers. None. But it doesn't seem that I could have climbed along the top of the cars. Was I *that* James Bond? In the snow and ice? I got back to him, but I really can't piece together how I did it. I couldn't have just Spider-Manned across the side of the car. So I must have got on top and crawled. Now we were together. Would we just stay there until we fell off together and died?

We decided to move toward the front of the train.

I guess we had to. I think we were crawling on top for like a half hour. We were so cold. It was so dark. And there were several engines. We got to one of the front engines and crawled down the frozen ladder to the door. The door was unlocked, and it was warm in there. It was just a big warm room with big loud engines all around and no people. We opened that door and the warm just hit us like an illegal paradise. Industrial warm. Like dangerous warm. I had prayed for warm, and it was going to hit me like a flaming monkey's paw.

"Are we going to get arrested? Shot?" Adam's fear had thawed out quickly.

"I don't know. It's warm. You know, like hot. Jesus."

"Can we be in here?"

"I can't imagine we're welcome. We're hippies. We aren't welcome anywhere. We really aren't supposed to be here."

"What do we do?"

We took off our clothes. We didn't strip naked, but we took off our cold coats and socks and pants and draped them over the hot engines. Someone who knows something about trains could probably figure where we were, but we were happy to be there. We were in our wet underwear and nothing else. It would have been a great time to shoot a gay porn scene. Wait just a fucking minute. Did I say somewhere we were seventeen years old and then suggest we should have fucked? Is this book now kiddie porn? Oops. Now I remember: we were both eighteen.

We had some food in our packs and we had our

sleeping bags, so we ate and laid the sleeping bags out and slept on top of them as dark, cold, wet Canada flew by us. We didn't know what direction we were going, but we were warm. That train was going fast. I guess it was about midnight. We were far away from Greenfield, and we were warm, and we fell asleep. We were tired hobos.

Bob Dylan never really did it, he never really hopped a train, but I really did. I really hopped a train. Arlo Guthrie never did it, but I really hopped a train. I would never do it again. Never. But I was riding someone's father's magic carpet made of steel. Goddamn.

CHAPTER 2

Either dawn's early light or our train slowing down woke us up at the same time. We were covered in sweat and our clothes were baked where they hung over some big metal thing. Totally baked, beyond toasty. We were rolling through a train yard. We got dressed. The freshly baked clothes sucked all the sweat off our bodies. We put our L.L.Bean down jackets back on. Now we were way too hot, like a Scandinavian sauna with metal rocks and no water. We rolled up our sleeping bags and reattached them to our packs.

While being way too hot, we were going to jump off a hot train into the cold snow and ice on frozen dirt in the train yard. Our point of view was Einstein shining a flashlight off the front of our freezing train to explain special relativity to Marilyn Monroe. We were speed-drunk. How fast were we going? We couldn't tell. We slid open the engine door. Jesus Christ. We were so hot, and the world was so cold. You know those Finnish crazy people who go from pizza-oven saunas to subzero salt water, because they have nothing else to do in the arctic circle? You know those people? They need to stop doing that. We were in our train sauna, and we were about to jump onto frozen dirt that was moving backward relatively really fast. Dylan and those blues guys singing about slow trains? This slow train was way too fast. Again, I jumped first. I didn't want to see Adam die before I had to jump.

Stuntpeople say you're supposed to roll when you hit. We didn't remember that stuntperson's rule, but there was a physics rule. Who needs a stunt rule? My feet touched the ground for an instant and the train momentum pulled the frozen dirt rug out from under me. I didn't just roll, I bounced. Jesus. Just bouncing and rolling, in every direction, ass over teakettle, over third base, over elbow. I was in a freezing-cold wet industrial dryer. Poor Adam, he had to watch me and then jump. I was surprised by what happened when I hit. Adam would be shocked that it was even worse than it looked.

The age I am now, when I stand up, after sitting for a while, everything hurts. My knees, my legs, my feet, my ankles, my chest, my neck, my arms, my wrists, my ass, my mind. Everything. My children can't understand how it can be that hard and painful to just stand up. Just to move. Well, a long time ago, when Dad was your age, he jumped off a fucking moving train onto frozen ground. He was put into a subzero lapidary tumbler with ice grit. That's one of the things that took the rough edges off Dad. Go ahead, children, get tattoos on your face, but don't jump off a speeding train on the tundra.

Adam and I lay there with our packs still attached, on the frozen railroad ground. Like frozen turtles with our bedclothes outside our shells. This was the time when some people liked to beat up hippies. Recently the Proud Boys tried to bring that back into fashion. We were scared. What if a Canadian railroad guy who listened to Merle Haggard saw us? Would he hit us with his special hippie-hitting train stick? We tried to stand up. We *could* stand up. We hurt bad but we could stand up. Damn, we probably could have fucked. At that point we could still hear and see clearly and remember names. It's wonderful to be seventeen, I mean eighteen, to be doing the damage instead of living with its consequences.

Adam and I were standing in a train yard somewhere in Canada. Sweating inside our hot clothes and freezing in the train-manufactured tundra. We started to sneak, as much as two huge hippies with backpacks, sleeping bags, and fluorescent bell-bottoms can sneak, out of the train yard. There were fences made to keep us out that were now keeping us in. We got over those. What's a few more cuts to our hands and bangs to our knees?

It was dawn in rural Canada. Like frozen Mayberry in a snow globe. There was no one around. It wasn't a train station; it was a train yard. Just nothing going on. We didn't know what direction we were from Chicago. We didn't know what direction we were from Montreal. We didn't know what direction we were from fuck.

"What's that over there?"

"I think it's a milk truck?"

"Did that train take us back to the 1930s?"

"It's a milk truck."

"Let's get a ride."

"Can you hitchhike on a milk truck?"

"Let's find out."

We ran across the street and stuck out our thumbs.

A nice Canadian (redundant) milkman didn't have to slow much to come to a full stop, he was sure slower than the slow train. We could have jumped on and climbed across his roof.

"Where ya going, eh?" (He *must* have said "eh.")

"Um, is there a highway nearby?"

"Yup, up the road a ways, get in."

The houses were pretty spread out. He stopped a few times to leave off lactose products while we waited in the truck. This is the days before cell phones. There was no one in the world who knew we were in a Canadian milk truck, except the Canadian milkman, and he didn't know me from Adam, in both senses. These days everyone knows where everyone is all the time. It wasn't that way for most of human history. Mr. Milkman dropped us at an on-ramp to something that passed for a freeway in Canada in 1973.

We never asked him where we were. We knew where we were, we were in a milk truck. But now it was time to figure out what town we were in, so we could get to Chicago. As the milk truck very slowly pulled away, we stood between on-ramps. We figured we probably had to go south, the USA is south of Canada, right? But "south" wasn't one of the choices. The choices were *est* or *ouest*. We figured we wanted *ouest*. But where were we?

This is a novel. I made a lot of this shit up. Well, I'm *going* to make a lot of shit up as the book goes on, but up to now, I'm just remembering. So far, it's all true, and right now you need to understand that, because I'm about to write something unbelievable. My buddy Neil Gaiman said, "Life is always going to be stranger than fiction, because fiction has to be convincing, and life doesn't." You know that Adam and I are stupid teenagers, but in fiction we couldn't be stupid enough for this next scene. This next scene is true. It's too wicked stupid to make up.

We could see a sign down on the freeway and we figured that would tell us where we were. We both wore glasses, little wire-rim granny glasses (exactly what I'm wearing now), but at that time our eyes were able to be fully corrected. I could read the sign. I read the sign and Adam pulled out the American Automobile Association map that my mom and dad had given us.

"Yeah, it says, 'Exit—Sortie.' See if you can find 'Sortie' on the map."

That's the truth—we looked at the map for a very long time trying the find the Canadian town of Sortie. A long time. We had nothing else to do, there were no cars coming. Not even the hope of a ride, so we just looked all over our map—"You scan this side of it, I'll take the other side." We weren't surprised we couldn't find the lovely hamlet of Sortie, we had no idea where to be looking on the map. We figured we were trying to find a needle-dick town in the giant haystack that was Canada. We had no luck.

But you don't need luck in Canada. People are just nice and helpful. It took fifteen minutes for the first car to go by us. But the second one stopped for us: "Where you going (eh)?"

"Chicago."

"What? Chicago? Where did you start, eh?"

"Massachusetts."

"What? How did you get way up here then, eh?"

"We don't know where we are. We couldn't find Sortie on the map."

"What? Sortie means 'exit' in French." *You idiots* was implied, *eh*.

"Oh, so that's why it was on the exit sign."

"Yeah, and that's why we couldn't find it on the map," Adam chimed in. We'd solved it!

The nice Canadian told us where we were. I don't remember now where we were, but we were way north, like crazy north. Way up where there were still milkmen near the sorties. We talked to our frozen hillbilly savior, and he drove us a ways south and we all figured that the train we hopped in Montreal carried us due north all night at train speed. We were way north.

I just talked to my friend Ron Gomes, who is Canadian, and more importantly can read a map and use the Internet. I told him this story, and he did all the work—work that I should have done for my own book—and this is what he figured (he's going with trains and highways that existed in 1973; he's careful):

Ron's guess—a northbound train all night from Montreal maybe took us to Val d'Or, a town in western Quebec, about 150 miles from the Ontario border. Val d'Or is a better name for a town than Sortie. The road where the milk truck left us could have been the Trans-Canada Highway to Ontario. We said to everyone who picked us up, "We're trying to get to Chicago," always relying on the kindness and navigation ability of strangers. The Canadians who picked us up might have taken us down until we joined Ontario Highway 11 heading south.

If the above was what happened, and that's possible, then Highway 11 might have taken us through North Bay and then to Barrie where we could have joined Highway 400 south to Vaughn, just north of Toronto, where we would have hitched Highway 407 southeast to the 401, which is a big important highway.

Strangers would have wanted to get us to the 401 to get us toward Chicago. The 401 could have brought us through Mississauga and some other Toronto suburbs and finally to Windsor. Windsor has great strip clubs and I have a few amazing sex stories from there, but those are from much later in my life and I probably won't be able to squeeze them in this book, because there's street juggling and a robbery to deal with.

After Windsor, if we were ever there, we might

have crossed the border, going north, into Detroit. There the I-96 would have been a quick ride to Livonia, Michigan, where the Michigan M-14 could have ridden us into Ann Arbor where we might have joined the I-94 which could have eventually taken us to the eastern shore of Lake Michigan and into Indiana, and then all the way to Chicago. That's about fifteen hours of driving, if you're not hitchhiking. Fifteen hours of continuous driving. To put this in perspective: driving directly from Greenfield, Massachusetts, without spending any time waiting on the side of the road with our thumbs out, to Chicago would be only fourteen hours. So, we spent twenty-four hours hitching and hopping a train, risking our lives traveling from Greenfield to get to Val d'Or, which put us an hour farther from Chicago than we would have been if we'd slept safely in our beds at home and left the next morning in the right direction. But then I would never have hopped a train. I could have just lied about it like Bob Dylan, like a Nobel Prize winner, instead of an idiot.

If this book ever comes out and I do a book tour, there might be a . . . let's call them "a very careful person," who reads to this point in the book and spends a lot of time researching and using a map. That "very careful person" will come up to me after my reading and tell me they think Adam and I really hopped a different train and took a different route, and they'll show the correct route to me on their phone and explain their reasoning. If someone does that, I will smile and nod and say, "Probably, thanks," and I will be very kind, but I won't give the slightest Windsor-strip-club fuck.

Adam was not a small hippie, but I was bigger. So, by the rules of the road, I got the front seat in a bunch of cars, and we got to Larburg in Chicago. We slept on his floor for two nights and then hitchhiked back. Moms and dads were very happy to see us. The train bruises faded.

CHAPTER 3

From spring break to graduation wasn't long, especially since I wasn't going to classes, no classes at Greenfield High. I was driving up to local colleges to sit in on classes and earning money selling ice cream from my guru's Ding Dong truck. I made more money to sew in my pack before I split. I was willing to disappoint my parents by not going to college, but I threw them the bone of going to my graduation. I graduated on a plea bargain. I had perfect SATs. When the scores came in, I went directly to our principal and said, "I got good SAT scores, right? Best GHS has ever had, right? And you know I can talk, right? So here's the deal: I'm not going to come to school again or do any work. None. And if I don't graduate, I will go in front of the school board, whip out my big fat hairy scores, and explain how you, sir, have let down the gifted students."

He asked if I was threatening him. I told him

I thought I'd made that clear. He told me to get out of his office. I didn't do another lick of work. I graduated at the bottom of my class, the very bottom; when he handed me my diploma onstage with my fluorescent bell-bottoms showing under the too-short gown, he gave me a look that certainly would have killed me dead if I had given the slightest fuck. Because of that sleezy, bully backroom deal, I graduated, and even at the bottom of my class my mom and dad were happy. They were good parents. I was a less-good son.

I sewed a few hundred into several different parts of my pack. (How does sewing into the backpack fabric help? If someone robs a hippie, don't they just take the whole pack? Who robs a hippie?) Anyway, I never used any of that money. If you're in the 01301 zip, go to Silver Street, I think the pack is still upstairs in the garage. I bet the pack is rotted by now and the money will just be falling out for you. The woman who lives there now isn't going to visit the creepy garage attic. (Now this book is one of those treasure-hunt-mystery things! I must remember to tell the publisher.) With the sewing done, I was ready to leave again, and my parents drove me to the same rotary by the Mohawk Trail Howard Johnson's. I was alone. Adam had gone off to study pottery, which out-hippied me, so I was alone.

This time my traveling weather was hot. I was alone by the side of the road, though still singing pop tunes. This wasn't a spring-break trip anymore; this was now officially my life. School was over. I had no plans. I was going to see America. Jack Kerouac didn't know how to drive, he couldn't drive, he didn't drive, and Bob Dylan didn't hop trains or work in carnivals (he might not even have been positive it was 4th Street), but I was about to spend maybe the rest of my life living Jack's and Bob's lies.

In the three months between spring break and graduation, a lot had changed. The biggest event was that I'd broken up with the love of my life, Jen. Our plan had been to move together to Paris to become the next Simone de Beauvoir and Jean-Paul Sartre. Her father woke us up from that dream when he made her stop banging a hippie and go to college. My revenge against her and her father was that I would never become a great writer (the one promise to myself that I've kept). Even worse in their eyes and my eyes at the time, I would be funny. Her dad really didn't respect funny at all. She didn't respect funny at all. I didn't respect funny at all. I didn't want to be funny. I wanted to be heavy, serious, and important. My whole life people have laughed at me, not *with* me, but I've never minded. I got used to it. I'd try to talk from my heart and people would laugh at me. Fine. I liked only Lenny Bruce as a comic because I thought his comedy was secondary to his ideas, which were serious, heavy, and important (like sniffing glue?). It was years before I realized that funny was Lenny's most important idea.

I had gotten into the Ringling Bros. and Barnum & Bailey Greatest Show on Earth Clown College (harder to get into than Harvard percentage-wise, and I was the last one picked). Pants-drop classes didn't start until fall, so I planned to hitchhike for three months, do Clown College for three months, and then hitchhike for another year or so. That was my plan. For most people, living homeless on the streets is not a plan, it's the failure of another plan. But homeless in America was my only plan. I figured at least it would be hard to fail at that.

No one uses the words *bum*, *tramp*, or *hobo* anymore. Even the word *homeless* has been replaced by *unhoused* and *houseless*. *Bum*, *tramp*, and *hobo* were already outdated by the time I was on the road, and I never heard them used to describe me (well, maybe *bum*). If I'd known the subtle differences, I would have self-identified as a hobo. A hobo travels and is willing to work, a tramp travels but avoids work, and a bum neither travels nor works.

Maybe I was a tramp because I sure avoided any honest work. After dishwashing and dealing ice cream in high school, I never did an honest day's work again. I juggled and told jokes on the street for money, but I didn't fucking wait on tables. I pretended to be a student and signed up for a lot of psychological tests at the University of Chicago at five bucks a pop, but that ain't working. I sure didn't dig any fucking ditches. I wasn't even honestly houseless; my mom and dad had a home they'd built themselves, just the two of them, and I was welcome to live there forever. I could be living there now, and I might be a lot happier. I had hundreds of dollars sewed in my pack (for reasons that are forgotten, but you can find that money by following clues hidden throughout this book). I wasn't a runaway, I was seventeen (eighteen in case there are sex scenes coming up), almost the age of majority, and I called my mom and dad, collect, from a phone booth every day. I had a home. I had money. I loved my mom and dad, they loved me, and they knew where I was. I talked to my mom, usually both my mom and dad, but at least my mom, every day that we were both alive. No matter what, I would find time to call home, and I got home every couple of months; I would hitchhike through and get my clothes really cleaned, my stomach really fed, and my heart really loved. I was running away from Greenfield, but I sure wasn't running away from my mom and dad. My dad died just a few months before my mom. They didn't die that young, yet they were too old when I was born. Not too old to love me and raise me, but too old to be there when my life fell apart. That's good. They got to be proud of me going to Ringling Bros. and Barnum & Bailey Greatest Show on Earth Clown College. You know, it ain't Harvard, it ain't what they wanted, but they had so much pride to give, they could spend it freely on their son being a fucking clown.

I wasn't a runaway. I don't know what word would describe me at that time, but soon I would be a street performer, and a good one. After a couple years I was one of the best. In terms of money, I might have been the best.

In my L.L.Bean lightweight, all-weather, you-can-climb-Everest-with-this-fucking-thing knapsack, I had juggling equipment. I had three twenty-inch-long pieces of broom handle, colorfully taped, with a colored rubber ball stuck and glued to one end of each. Those were my juggling clubs ("real" juggling clubs took up too much room and were too expensive). In addition to the huge balls I had to have swinging to do all this, I also had juggling balls. At that time juggling was not a college-jock thing like it would become several years later. Special-order beanbag juggling "balls" just weren't available. There weren't any juggling supply companies. I just had a bunch of lacrosse balls, both white and fluorescent-orange, although soon they'd all be dirty enough to look almost the same color. Dog balls were a slightly better size and weight for juggling, but they made my hands smell funny (make up your own goddamn joke).

I didn't need to spend money. I'd just meet someone who would let me sleep on the couch or I'd fuck someone and sleep with them, or, in rare cases, I'd use my sleeping bag. I'd lie down somewhere outside and wait for lawn sprinklers to rudely wake me up and I'd laugh. I was that kind of hippie. I made friends quickly and easily, and I fucked a lot, so I usually had a place inside to sleep. I didn't need money for smokes, drinks, or drugs because I never did any of that. I was six foot seven and weighed 180 pounds so food seemed optional, and nothing seemed dangerous.

I'd pull out my clubs and balls on any street or campus, put out my metaphorical hat, do some juggling, tell some jokes, and I'd make more than enough for a slice of apple pie and a chocolate milkshake before the police or security threw me out. That jingle would last me until at least the next day, sometimes for a week. There was always leftover pizza in the dorms people snuck me into. I had more money than the college students I was crashing with and fucking. I had no expenses.

It's easy to get on college radio. They had more time to fill than they had albums by Can and Magma. I would find the station and show up and let them interview a real peripatetic street juggler. I'd try to be funny (I had started to respect that skill), and I'd say that anyone who called in to the station, I'd teach them to juggle in exchange for pizza. People would call in. I got good at teaching juggling, sharing stories, and eating pizza.

My hitchhiking developed into just going from college to college. I often got picked up by college students who were on their way back to school, so I went along. It's easy to travel when you have no destination. I could juggle anywhere for a few bucks, and colleges were where there were women my age. The women were all reading or listening to people who lied about hitchhiking, and I was doing it for real. I didn't have a guitar, but I had balls. I'd stay a few days. Usually until I met someone driving somewhere interesting, or sometimes just driving somewhere else. Once you get to the middle of the country, it can be several miles between interesting. While I was on campus, I'd sign up for a shrink study (that's why I don't trust those studies), go on the radio, even sit in on a class or two. I'd go to any bar that had live bands in the evening and see if I could do ten minutes before the music set to warm up the crowd. I often sucked, and the patrons liked booing me. But every time I did a show, I sucked a little less. I was getting better.

Someone called in to a radio show I was on one day and said they'd buy me a pizza if I taught a whole party to juggle. They wanted me to teach everyone they knew how to juggle. I got the address and headed over. It was a big house close to campus. I don't remember what campus. I don't remember what state. I probably didn't know where I was at the time. I might have thought I was in Sortie. I showed up and they told me it was a nude party. Oh boy. I took off all my clothes immediately and pulled out my balls. Naked is the only way to look more hippie than tie-dye. Long hair, super-skinny bodies, and big hairy patches (this was the seventies).

There were a few dozen people, and they were all naked. It was nice. There were a lot of drugs involved, and that did make my students more difficult to teach. I don't know what drug they were indulging in, but it was a drug that diminished both hand-eye coordination and focus. Some people still learned.

My mom took me to a juggling convention when I was about fifteen and I met my first real professional juggler. He was Southern and shy and had one joke he told over and over: "I had a girlfriend back home who used to juggle topless . . . looked like she was doing five . . . it was an optical illusion of course."

If that joke is told with good delivery and timing, it's not a good joke. If it's told with bad delivery and timing, it's a great joke. I was teaching college women to juggle naked . . . so I had visual reinforcements. I told that topless-juggling joke carefully badly and exactly out of rhythm and it killed. Told like that while everyone is nude, the joke is fucking Lenny Bruce at Carnegie Hall. The bad thing about naked parties is that unless it's billboarded on the invitations as an orgy, there's often less sex than at a clothed party—everyone is trying to prove that nudity doesn't have to be about sex. That's like trying to convince me dinosaurs played table tennis; I don't buy it. But I taught juggling and ended up having a great time, even though it was a shitty frozen pizza. Funny what a fellow remembers. Any good conversations? What state was it in? Did I fuck that night? Don't know. Don't know. Don't know. Was it a good pizza? No.

I continued to live like Bob Dylan didn't. I made very few decisions. I got picked up by a guy in Nebraska, in a big fancy car. He said, "Set the cruise control for ninety and wake me up when we're near LA." So, I went to LA. There was an attractive woman in LA who wanted to hitch to Florida, but she was afraid of being a woman hitchhiking alone, so I traveled with her. I got rides a lot faster with her. By being together, I looked less scary to drivers, and she looked less of a whore. Together we were a loving young couple out to see America.

The second time a gun was pulled on me was because of her. We got picked up by a real outcast. Today he would be an incel, and he would have a supportive peer group to belong to, but back then he was just a creep on his own, not part of a more dangerous creep society. He offered us a place to stay and when we got there, he pulled a rifle on me and said he was going to sleep with Cindy. I think if you're using a gun to commit rape, you shouldn't have to use a euphemism, but what the fuck do I know? I said no he wasn't and that I would attack him with a knife. It was a complete bluff—I couldn't fucking attack an annoying housefly with an old newspaper, let alone attack a man with a knife. That remains true today even after my brushes with the law. All a bluff, but I puffed up like an impotent puffer fish. He dropped the gun. Unlikely that he had any real intention of using it anyway, but it didn't feel that way to me. To me it was a gun pointed at me. I grabbed his dropped old rifle off the floor and went fucking nuts. I checked to make sure the weapon wasn't loaded and then used it like a baseball bat to smash up his house. There was some adrenaline I needed to burn off. I sure wasn't going to hurt him, I've never hurt anyone, but I smashed up his gun and smashed the shit out of his house. The gunsight cut my hands and I didn't even feel it until the next day. I had a bloody gun, and this was before what I'd end up doing a few years later. I put him in a room, or maybe a closet, I don't really remember, and put things in front of the door so it would be hard and loud for him to get out of there.

Cindy and I slept in his house, with him right there in a room behind a refrigerator covered in pans with his TV on top. That night I earned the Cindy strain of herpes. Cindy and I got up the next morning and had a romantic breakfast from his dented refrigerator while he screamed and cried behind the same fridge, then we left the dirty dishes and him behind the refrigerator and I got Cindy to Florida safely.

During those couple years on the road, with my clown sabbatical in the middle, I went back and forth and up and down the USA a few times in each direction. I saw America. I saw the inside of biker clubhouses. I was part of weird psych experiments on college campuses. I went to jail for a night. I even saw the inside of Scientology. Why did they let me in there? Scientology rips people off, that's what it was designed for. Why would you try to rip off a hippie? Why beg a dirty hippie to come into your center? Why try to scam him? The street grunt told me I could take an IQ test, do some filing for them, and they'd give me lunch. I could have just juggled and bought my own fucking lunch, but I wanted to hear the whole crazy-ass Scientology sales pitch firsthand—I like crazy, and I always enjoy the opportunity to arrange files in random order to fuck up a cult. I ate their food, messed up their files good, and laughed at their jive. I guess that means I passed their intelligence test.

CHAPTER 4

By 1976 I was still street performing but now I was a very successful street performer. How successful can you be as a street performer? You might be surprised. I'd cut my hair. I now wore white pants and a Hawaiian shirt when I juggled on the streets. Many street performers think their job is related to begging and they should look like they need the money. I thought the opposite, I thought I'd make more money if they believed I was very successful. If I made them embarrassed to give me change. I thought looking well-off would make the value of the bills go up.

I wore a Hamilton Pulsar P1, the first digital watch to hit the market. It showed the time on a red light–emitting diode display, with a synthetic ruby crystal and a real gold case. I had to push a button to get a flash of the time and for a moment my wrist glowed like a robot from way in the future, like 2029. We didn't really have to wait that long. Within a few years digital watches were given away in cereal boxes. But in 1976 that watch cost me over two grand, which in today's dollars would be over two grand. It's the same goddamn number! If numbers changed with time, our universe would make even less sense. But in terms of buying power, two grand was about fifteen grand. I was a street performer with the same watch James Bond wore in *Live and Let Die*, and I hadn't boosted it. I bought it, in cash. That cash was over two thousand one-dollar bills. I collected lots of twenties and even a hundred now and again with my juggling, but I liked to buy the most expensive things in dirty one-dollar bills. At some level it was a fuck you to all the squares. It represented that I was a sibling to the strippers and pole dancers, even though my crumpled folding money didn't smell as good as theirs. I bought that Pulsar even before I started making serious do-re-mi. I bought it before I was working Philly. The biggest change since my hitchhiking days was that I'd lost my voice. I could still scream and do shows, and I was still about thirty logarithmic decibels louder than fuck, but I couldn't talk in a normal voice anymore. I had a raspy whisper, and I had a big strong scream, but nothing in between. My throat was sore all the time. I carried Chloraseptic local anesthetic with me. I had the lozenges too but mostly I used the spray and sometimes I drank the spray. It was a disgusting and very unhealthy habit, yet it came with the job of screaming like a nut.

I had rented a house in Trenton with a couple guys

I'd met. We wanted to start a small theater company in Philly. We weren't ever going to make money doing theater, so I would support us doing street shows. I wouldn't be traveling anymore, so I wanted to find a good place to settle in, do shows, and bring the bacon from every week.

I've always had weird rules for myself. I had worked a few small Renaissance faires (thou must add the "e"), carnivals, and arts festivals, but I didn't like that anymore. I had decided to only juggle on the streets where it was illegal. *"To live outside the law you must be honest"*—something else Bob Dylan sang and maybe didn't live. I wanted to be an outlaw. That's easier than I thought at the time; I could have gotten there even without doing a show.

I was sniffing around for a place where street juggling was not legal but where I could still make a lot of money. Head House Square was a historic site in Philly, and they'd just built New Market. It was a place with upscale yuppie stores (people were in the market to buy yuppies back then), fancy bars, and restaurants. They had water features with a stage for fluffy-haired women to do adult contemporary covers, along with a guy with a beard and glasses on a Fender Rhodes. I didn't want to work the stage, there was no money there, but there was a prime place where people came in out of the shopping/restaurant area. A big grand entrance with open space. There was a construction wall I could use as my backdrop to make me look a little funky, and there were big stairs where people could stand and see me over the heads of the closer people. I figured I could do a few hundred people there, maybe five hundred a show, and probably do five shows on Friday, ten on Saturday, and five more on Sunday. Twenty weekend shows for yuppies would make me more than enough jingle. Is there such a thing as "more than enough" money? I thought so, but the rest of the story will show I didn't totally believe that.

There were a couple problems to overcome in Head House. First the police. I didn't want it to be legal, but I wanted to get away with it. The reason police bust street performers is local businesses rat them out. Shop owners call the police to take out the street trash. I nipped that in the bud. I went to every store and restaurant and bought stuff. I bought yuppie bullshit trinkets and threw them away. I bought flowers and gave them to the woman working the hot dog stand hoping it would help get me laid. I took friends to supper at all the restaurants.

I introduced myself to every owner and manager I could find: "My name is Poe, I'm a street juggler and I want to start doing shows right over there. I'm hopeful I can get big crowds moving through here and help us all out. But I want everyone to be happy, so please, if you feel I'm hurting your business in any way, you just let me know, and I'll move or do whatever else I can do to help." I said that and then checked with each of them after all my early shows. I could make them happy. No complaints to the police, all complaints to me—that was the goal. It was easier than I thought. They seemed to like me and understand.

Then there were the police themselves. Whenever I saw cops I'd go over: "Hi, I'm a street juggler. I know that begging and vagrancy is illegal. I'm going to be doing a show right over there and I'd love you to stop by and watch. I think I do a good show and I hope you like it. Please watch the show and if you think I'm begging, please bust me, that's your job. But if you think I do a good show, well, pay me, tip me, because I deserve it. I'm not a beggar. And here's my driver's license as ID." It was ballsy, but a lack of balls was never my problem. One officer said that his child was into juggling and magic. The next day I showed up with a couple of magic tricks that I had bought at a local shop. Is that a bribe? Yes. It was the cost of doing my business.

Once the businesspeople and police were all fixed, there was the bigger problem. There was a gang that hung out there. "Gang" is the wrong word. They were children. Latino boys, tweens, and young teenagers. Other street performers had tried this prime area (we can all smell yuppie coin), but this gang of children harassed them during the shows, yelling, swearing, and grabbing focus. That wasn't all they grabbed; they stole props whenever the performers turned their backs even for a second. They made it impossible to work.

I had a plan for dealing with them. It was at least risky, probably stupid, but who cares? My act then included juggling huge knives. I carried them stuck in a big rustic log. My show ended with me juggling knives blindfolded and then juggling knives around a blindfolded audience member. She was blindfolded with the same opaque (yeah, sure) black bag I put over my head as a blindfold, so everyone knew I couldn't see (I could) and was juggling blind (I wasn't). Putting it over the audience member's head showed that the blindfold was legit (nope), and it gave me a big black bag that would soon be filled with money. I couldn't pass a hat; I needed more money than would fit in a hat. I wanted big bags of money. I knew that as soon as I started my first show (which started with ball juggling), my beautiful, custom-made, expensive juggling knives and the blindfold would be gone to the modern Latino equivalent of the Spanky and Our Gang clubhouse with the *No Girlz Allow3d* sign.

My plan was stupid, but I thought it just might work. As I set down my props for my first show, the children immediately started gathering around to fuck me up. I turned to the one who looked like the leader. I took my watch off and whisper/croaked, "Hi, my name is Poe, what's your name?"

"José. Why you talk like that?"

"Nice to meet you, José. I don't have a choice; my voice is fucked. Hey, could you do me a favor? I'm going to be doing a juggling show here and I don't like to juggle with my watch on and I can't have stuff in my pockets. It's an expensive watch, and I don't have anyone I know around here to take care of it while I juggle." I took my watch off and held it out. "Could you just hold on to it and keep it safe while I do my show?"

It was quite a gamble. I placed James Bond's

watch in José's hand. He pushed the button, and it lit his face up with the time. This might be the last time I'd see the watch, but on the streets, you gotta gamble to make money.

With José holding my watch, I smiled, said thanks, and turned away to start my show. At the end of it, all my props were there, and José ran over with my watch—"Here you go. Good show, Poe. You're funny."

By the third show of my second night, I'd finish my money collection and just throw the whole bag of money to José and his troops, so I could talk to folks with my hands empty. They would take the money, separate it out, sort it, and keep it safe. It turned into our groove. My final show every night I'd reach into the bag of my last take before it was sorted, and pass them a handful of money as their pay for helping me out. They bought (stole) the apples I used for every show in my act and always had all my props ready. They stored my props somewhere, took care of the money, and held my watch. I like to feel a watch on my wrist when I juggle, but I had to keep that naked-wrist lie going for all my time at Head House.

I ran all the street performing at Head House. There was Fat Jake, who played harmonica and spoons. He was way older than me, covered in tattoos before they were fashionable: sailor and jailhouse ink. He didn't make a lot of coin, though he also didn't stop traffic, so he could work between my shows easily without a problem. He blew harp okay, yet Jake was a drunk and very unhealthy. Twice I had to 911 his ass and ride with him in the ambulance to the hospital. He lived through both of the heart attacks he had on my watch. I looked out for Fat Jake.

The others who performed at Head House, I just made sure they wouldn't piss off the shop owners and cops, or otherwise get in the way of my do-re-mi. There were a couple magicians who weren't good for business, or I just plain didn't like, and José brought me all their props and they were gone after one show. Fuck them, there's a lot of streets in the world, get off my dick.

Once, a string quartet came down, music students who wanted to try "busking." None of us called it that, but they did. They were cute. They were good. I liked them. They didn't talk to me or even look around when they got there. They made no attempt to understand the situation, they just set up and started playing. I went over to listen and watch. They played for forty minutes. I eyeballed the money in their fiddle case. In forty minutes, they'd made forty-two dollars and almost half of that was a twenty from me. They took a break, and I went over and introduced myself.

"Hey, guys, you sound good, I loved it," I frog-whispered.

"Thanks."

"Yeah. My name is Poe, and I'm the juggler here. I work right over there doing street shows. And we should figure out our schedules, so we can all work together."

"No thanks, you just juggle and we'll do our music, okay?" He was snotty enough to be first violin. He was going to do all the talking. The other three just stood behind him. Pecking order matters in the string-quartet farmyard.

"See, the problem is that I'm wicked loud," I said. He looked at me skeptically. "It's a different voice when I'm working. When I'm working, I'm very loud, and I get big crowds, so if I start up while you're playing, I'll come off as rude unless I wait until you're done, and you just did forty minutes. I can't work with that."

"We are musicians. We're at the conservatory, and we're going to do this on weekends to make a little extra money. Serious musicians. Is a juggler trying to tell us how we should play music?" I think the viola player might have nodded in agreement, fucking toady.

"I'm a serious juggler and I'm not commenting on the music, I'm commenting on the venue. We have our little street-performing ecosystem here and it's working nicely, and I'd like to fold you in."

"So you're the boss here?" The cello player made a questioning face. The second violin was still trying to stay invisible.

"Listen—you just did forty minutes and made ten bucks apiece. I could have done two twelve-minute hunks and snagged over five hundred bucks. Fat Jake needs to do his five minutes, and we've got Abe Cadabra also working. We need to all get along here. I can make that happen." I could have paid them forty dollars an hour to *not* play. Musician subsidy.

"Fuck off."

"Hey, Paganini, you don't want to fuck with me, you really don't. I mean you really fucking don't. Look me in the eyes then look around here." They didn't even have the street sense to look around when I told them to. None of them checked their six. It seems at the conservatory it's rare for gangs of children to sneak up on string quartets. They didn't even see me hold my hand up to José and his troops to keep them back.

"Maybe we do want to fuck with you, juggle-boy, fuck off."

"I'm going to start a show right now, right here, a very special show, and you're going to stay and watch." I nodded to José. (No mind reading or secret codes, I'd talked to José before talking to the quartet. We had a flow chart on how it might go if they weren't nice.) They weren't nice and we had a plan.

"No thanks. We're not big juggling fans." The dismissive fuck. Cello chick chuckled and bounced in her black dress.

"I think you'll find it compelling. I bet you stay until the end." What happened next happened fast. Even twenty-year-old music students forget how fast tweens move. José's troops grabbed all the cases off the ground, and then the cello and the viola right out of their hands. They left the cheap folding chairs. At the same time, I made my move fast and rough. No mercy. I grabbed the wannabe concert master's violin by the neck, ripped it out of his hands, and held it over my head. He didn't expect that. If he tried to grab it away, we'd break his axe together. The quartet now had one violin among them. I had to remember to give José shit for being slower than a second violinist, but they'd grabbed enough to get the quartet's full attention. I was feeling the weight and balance of the violin in my hand. The quartet was about to see one of my best shows.

Time to start. I spit out the lozenge. I coughed up a huge glob of bloody mucus, spat that at the fiddler's feet (I didn't hit him, didn't try), gave a quick yell, and my voice changed. When I was working, I was loud. I was working and I was loud and clear, "Hey everyone," at full performance volume, right in the first chair's face, "I'm going to do a special juggling show over here. Let's get a crowd. I need a crowd. C'mon, you don't want to miss this. I'm about to do a juggling show. I'm going to juggle knives, eat an apple while juggling, and for my spectacular finish I will juggle this . . ." I looked the violist in the eye, "valuable violin . . ." I looked again, "priceless violin." I said quietly to him, "Sorry, showbiz hyperbole, I know your dad knows exactly what he paid for it, and what it's worth now."

A crowd formed right away. A big crowd. The troops had set up my knives, balls, apple, and hood in my usual place across the street. The musicians' cases had disappeared into the clubhouse with the other priceless string instruments. I walked over to my usual spot, pattering all the way. I was surprised at how many violin jokes I came up with, holding the instrument high over my head, repeating how precious it was and how I was going to juggle it at the end of my show. I led the crowd across the street. When I was near my props, I handed the fiddle to José. The first-chair asshole had even less of a chance of getting it back in one piece from José. The first violinist had no choice but to watch the first juggler.

I did a great show. Eleven minutes in, after a lot of hype about the danger of the knives and the value of the violin, I juggled two of my knives along with the fiddle while blindfolded. Usually, the blindfold juggle was the relaxing time of the show. A time to reflect. It was intense.

The trick was nothing, juggling my three knives was something I could almost do blindfolded, and I wasn't really blindfolded. I could see clearly. There was no patter, it was heavy, it was my big-dick finish. During that trick, I was alone in the invisibility of a fake blindfold. I would look through the juggle and look out at the crowd. I could see my audience, in public, when they thought I couldn't see them. There is a story in some carny book about a woman's first job in a cooch show. A cooch show is a tent in the carnival where women strip after the show. What happens in there changes from county to county, depending on how well the "patch" on the show has greased the local officials (often having one of the cooch performers doing a more organic grease). It's a traveling "gentlemen's club." "Gentleman's club" is the best example of a dysphemism. Take the perfectly clear, beautiful, and sweet term "titty bar," and make it something that forces you to think of unhealthy cigars instead of nice healthy breasts. So this young woman went out her first time to strip naked at the cooch show in front of strangers. She did her hunk and came back freaked out and crying. When one of the other performers came to comfort her, she said, through her sobs, "I knew they were going to see me naked, I didn't know I'd have to see *them*." She could have added the word "naked" to the end of that sentence. When I looked through the hood as I juggled, I was seeing people watching a show. I'd look at attractive women and let my eyes wander wherever they wanted. The juggler was gone, out on his own, and I was there to float and stare. I could really watch people watching me. It was a slight, but moral violation of their privacy. It was dirty and peaceful.

That was with three knives. With two knives and the asshole's violin, it was different. I really didn't want to fuck up. I didn't get to space out. I stayed right there, watching the violin and the knives and making sure I was perfect. The violin was safe. I didn't watch the audience watching, but I knew I was killing. It was a good trick. A *great* trick, and the audience sure seemed to enjoy it. We'd see just how good the show was after I did my collection.

I handed the violin back to José and passed among the cheering crowd, giving them a chance to drop their appreciation into my executioner's hood/blindfold/collection purse. At the end I didn't throw the money-filled bag to José. I held onto it, carried it over to the violinist and opened the bag in front of him, and, in my nonperforming frog-croak-whisper, said: "See that, that's about four hundred and twenty-five bucks. I got that doing my tight twelve with a special ending. If you had been raised properly and were respectful and polite, you could be working here with us . . . and . . . you can *still* work with us if you can find some humility."

Joshua Bell stayed silent. José brought over his violin. Jascha Heifetz was afraid to reach for it. José handed the violin to me. I looked it over carefully.

A few minutes after a show, my voice was at its worst. I could barely whisper, and my throat hurt so bad. I took a swig of Chloraseptic, handed the bottle back to José, and looked over the violin. "Seems fine. I'm a good juggler. No drops and I caught it gently every time. You'll need to check your bridge and sound post; I hope they weren't jostled. I don't think you'll need a luthier, but make sure you have it checked out. You'll probably have to tune it before your next show, sorry."

I carefully handed his violin back. All the other instruments and cases appeared out of nowhere and went to their owners. Everything was in fine condition. The quartet stomped off and we never saw them again. It was a great story that I knew I'd be telling as long as I was Poe, but I felt bad. The music students were the dicks, but now I was the super dick. It didn't feel as good as it should have. Or it felt exactly as good as it should have. I was just a bully. You can't fucking win.

CHAPTER 5

I think our street magician, Abe Cadabra, might have been busted for diddling children or something like that. Something bad. I never saw him again. When a magician disappears for reals, it often means he's in stir, and usually for something creepy. Magicians don't shoplift or cheat the IRS. Abe was gone, and the next week, by chance, a new magician was there waiting for me when I arrived Friday.

Some magicians wear old-fashioned evening clothes and even capes. Some carry canes and wear top hats. It all started because of a French magician named Robert-Houdin. The "Houdin" part is where Erik Weiss got the name "Houdini." Robert-Houdin was a heavy cat. He invented the modern magician—not just the tricks and the style, but even the very idea of a modern magician as showbiz and not wizbiz. Magicians before him in the nineteenth century didn't simply dress like Asians or wizards because those clothes have a lot of sneaky pockets, they were pretending to be something jive-ass exotic and racist and hiding behind the jive. They acted like they were real magic, even worse than the bullshit "street magicians" of the 1990s.

Robert-Houdin got the idea of dressing just like his audience, which meant tails and opera hats. Robert-Houdin dressing in formal evening clothes was braver than Dylan going electric. Every magician followed suit—a hundred and fifty years later they hadn't noticed that their audiences weren't dressing like that anymore; they didn't want to notice because they had found good places to hide shit in those tailcoats, and rabbits looked good coming out of those hats.

These out-of-date-by-more-than-a-century costumes are one of the reasons magicians look stupid and can't get laid. Remember, this is a juggler writing this. The first time I saw our new magician, B.L. Herman, at Head House, I understood a different way of seeing those clothes. B.L. was dressed in that way, but not like a loser magician, more like a rhythm & blues or funk star. B.L. had a cape, but not an opera cape—a James Brown cape. His hat wasn't an opera hat, either—it was a top hat, like Screamin' Jay Hawkins or Little Richard might wear. Neither Jay nor Richard would ever wear a hat, their hair was too perfect, but they would have both dug B.L.'s hat. Also, his wardrobe wasn't black. I guess it was powder-blue, though it was hard to see the fabric through all the rhinestones. Even his shoes were glitter and rhinestones. He was wearing this costume on the street. These were real street clothes for my idea of the streets. B.L. was dressed like a superstar, not a cruise-ship magician. Before he said a word, I loved him.

"You Poe?"

"Yeah, the juggler."

"You okay? Your voice sounds fucked up and you stink of Vicks or something."

"Yeah, I'm fine." I didn't sound fine. I wasn't fine. I was coughing up blood.

"Okay, I'm B.L. Herman, I hope in a few weeks you'll be calling me Bee. I'm a magician. So, you got the cops and gangs juiced here, right? What do I pay you to work?"

"Nothing. No one takes a taste. You might tip out José and the troops, but that's your choice. We all work together to keep the cool."

"You wanna see my show first?"

"Are you as good as your shoes?"

"Better. Wanna see something?" He pulled out a deck of cards. They were well used, but the backs glittered to match his fucking shoes.

"Nah, you don't audition for me, just do your thing, keep the people happy, and don't piss off police or store owners. How do you work?"

"I'm in the center of a circle of people. I want them all around me. I don't do a show, I just kind of work."

"How long at a pop?"

"I just keep going, I can keep people around for as long as I want. I don't do patter, I sing, no words, just scat. I'd like to just stay way over there and keep working. I'm not too loud and I make bank the whole time."

"Yeah, that'll fuck up my shit. I do my two-minute crowd-gathering, then a twelve-minute show, and then about three minutes more to get my coin. Then I like the crowd to move on. So I kind of need twenty and then I start fresh the next hour. I can't do it with you over there because I'm loud. I'll look like an asshole yelling while you're working."

"I don't want to bust on a new friend, but you ain't loud, I can barely hear you and I'm right in your face smelling your hospital breath. You sound like Miles Davis on a bad day, and what are you drinking? You fucked up?"

"I blew my voice out doing what I do. I can't talk normal volume anymore. I either do the Miles thing or I scream. I got no in-between. When I'm working, I'm stupid-crazy loud, but I got nothing quiet. And what I'm drinking is Chloraseptic."

"Get you high?"

"No, it's a local anesthetic for my pipes. I got a wicked sore throat all the time. Killer. Listen, I do my twenty, give Fat Jake ten to bang spoons, play harp, and do his weird shit, and then you take up the rest of the hour until you give Jake another five before me. Cool? I'll watch your show and if you suck, I'll think of some way to get you to fuck off with kindness." I gestured to José, who came running over. "José, this is Mr. Herman, B.L. Herman. Sir, this is José. You asked who ran the streets here, it's José. We perform at his pleasure. José, B.L. is okay with us. Don't let anyone fuck with him."

B.L. addressed José: "Nice to meet you, you can call me Bee." He reached into some pocket somewhere in his funky Liberace suit and pulled out his glitter deck. "You got a favorite card, José?"

"Favorite card?"

I translated: "Name a card, José."

"Ace of spades?"

"That's too easy, I keep that one on top." B.L. turned the top card over, it was the ace of spades. "Make it hard."

"Wow, that's the card, wow."

"Name a hard one."

"I don't fucking know, five of diamonds." While they were talking, Bee was shuffling and cutting, it looked like a nervous habit, though it wasn't, he was doing the work.

Bee tilted his head with a questioning look, gestured for José to hold his hand out flat, and dealt the ace of spades facedown on the kid's hand. "I'm sorry, I didn't hear you. You're mumbling and croaking like your juggling frog-boy Poe over here. What card did you name?"

José spoke loudly and clearly: "Five of diamonds!"

"Okay, five of diamonds. Five of diamonds. I don't know as I have a five of diamonds." Bee looked through the deck, letting José see the cards too. There was no five of diamonds in the deck. "Nope. Wait." Bee did a big flourish with the cape, like James Brown or a glittery funk Dracula. The cape moved perfectly.

He must have practiced the cape move more than his card stack and top change put together. "What card you holding?"

"Ace of spades."

"Not anymore, my friend, take a look."

It was, of course, the five of diamonds. José had seen a real miracle. He didn't need me to tell him to take care of Bee.

That was the groove for the rest of the summer and into fall. I'd do my show, Fat Jake would blow harp for wine change, and Bee would do his thing.

Bee's thing was good. It was very good. Like nothing I'd ever seen. There was no beginning or end, it was all middle. He would stand in an open area and start twirling his cape. As people came to look, he'd start doing this weird funk groove with his mouth. This was years before beatbox, but that's kind of what he was doing, with notes in it and on top of it. He would start with a beat and then sing a bass line. The overdubbing was all done in the audiences' heads. He'd do the beat long enough that everyone had it, and then start singing the funk bass that would go over that beat. The audience had to put it together themselves. They had to remember the beat and lay the bass over it. With Bee they just did it. That alone was a miracle.

After he had the groove, he would start singing lead parts, kind of organ, and horns, and lead guitar, all with his mouth and all over the rhythm section that was now only in the punters' heads. He did this all while performing card tricks, coin tricks, hand magic, all executed perfectly. He was so fucking clean. Not one unnatural move and he was wearing a cape. He didn't work the crowd; Bee didn't seem to know there was a crowd there. He worked a group of three or four while the rest of the circle watched, yet his focus wasn't on anyone but the little chosen group. There was no one else in the world. He never spoke, he just had this solo-funk-band thing going, all laid down in everyone's head. He'd come back to rhythm and then to bass, just to remind people, to keep it going. He had a pro-singer voice with amazing range. Like those 1940s vocal groups, the Ink Spots or the Mills Brothers, who impersonated band instruments, but he was alone and doing funk. Musically it was very sophisticated and had such grooves. Everything fit his magic. He would do his own stings, flourishes, builds, and punches.

It wasn't silent but the magic was all mime. He'd get people to name cards, or guess which hand the coin was in, and he did it all without using words. All his props were off the body, from the suit. When he finished a routine for a little group, he would rub his fingers together—the universal symbol for *money*—and swing around and open his cape. He had a pouch there, bright red, contrasting with the rest of his outfit, and people would just drop tips in there. He'd nod a thank you, build up the groove, spin the cape again, and go to another group. Everyone was waiting for his attention and every group got a couple special tricks and a special groove.

He'd do that for about a half hour (that's all I let

him do). He'd hit about ten groups in that time and do between five and twenty dollars from each mini-show. He was doing about a buck and a half a show. We'd do about four rotations every Friday night and Sunday afternoon and then ten rounds on Saturday. After tipping out José and the troops, he was taking twenty-five hundred dollars out of Head House every weekend. That's good bread now, but in 1976 a very good living. I did about twice that, and Fat Jake could stay fat and drunk. We had a nice thing going and I finally did get to fuck the hot dog woman, and a few others who I scoped through my blindfold. I thought this would be my life.

CHAPTER 6

I don't know what Bee did during the week, but I worked with the theater group I was starting with my housemates in Trenton. I bought lights and a PA. I didn't know what to do with the PA. I had no idea how to find my voice in the theater. I didn't have an indoor voice. Was I going to scream like a freak or was I going to croak a whisper onstage. You might be imagining Tom Waits. Nope, compared to me, Tom sounded like Celine Dion. I had no voice that was usable in a theater.

I was living outside the law, and I was trying to be honest. I didn't have health insurance. If I needed doctoring, I just paid cash. I was twenty-two years old, what could go wrong? My voice first. My throat had already gone wrong, I'd fucked that up, for serious. I found the voice doctor who treated the real opera singers in Philly and made an appointment. I showed up coughing blood and drinking anesthetic. You would think the receptionist at a fancy voice place would be used to fucked-up voices, right? Not mine, she was freaked. My spitting globs of blood into Kleenex also bugged her. She got me into the doc. I told him I was carny trash and I screamed outdoors all the time.

He said, "How do you scream with this voice?"

"It's all I *can* do."

"You can scream?"

"Bet your ass. I do drink a lot of Chloraseptic."

"You're not supposed to drink that."

"I know."

"Let me take a look at your larynx."

"Sure."

He had this Roto-Rooter thing he was going to snake up my nose and down my throat. Nowadays they have cameras with lights on them, but this just had a scope on it, some newfangled fiber-optic thing with an eyepiece. He told me gently what he was going to do.

"Ain't no thang. Just do it. I've done blockhead, which is sticking nails up my nose, and sword-swallowing." No patient before me had ever practiced more for this procedure. He stuck it up my nose and then I throated the whole thing like seventies gay porn.

"Jesus Christ," he said, and doctors aren't supposed to say that. He told me to say "eeeeeee." I couldn't make a sound. He had me try again a few times; I finally got just a little vibration going. Not too impressive.

He whipped it out, which in this case could mean

he was so impressed with my throating he wanted to give me less of a challenge with his little doctor dick, but I just mean he pulled the long metal glowing Martian cock out of my throat and nose.

Careful readers are going to realize that the scope wasn't going down the same pipe as a throated dick, and right and double right—but it's the same no-puking skill. You would know by going up my nose and into my voice box that you could fuck my throat with impunity. Same skill set.

He asked if he could bring his colleague in to check it out, so I nosed and throated the scope again for his buddy. They were duly impressed with my damage. They took some pictures.

"Hey, you keep bringing people in, I'm going to charge them a quarter a pop to see the gross-out. How bad is it?"

"It's bad."

"What can I do?"

"Vocal rest. You need to stop screaming. You're going to keep doing damage and soon you won't have a voice."

"You mean like Tom Waits." *Small Change* had just come out, and I doubt the doc knew who I was talking about, but context gave him the idea.

"I mean like Marcel Marceau." We love funny doctors.

"What do you mean?"

"I mean you're close to not having a voice at all, at any volume."

"What do I do?"

"It's not what you do, it's what you *don't* do. Don't scream. As a matter of fact, don't talk. Complete vocal rest. You got two broken legs and you're still running a marathon every day."

"What can you do to fix it?"

"Nothing. You must stop. It's that easy."

"You mean it's that hard."

"You've got to stop. And you can't drink Chloraseptic. That's going to give you another whole set of problems. Probably has already done damage to your liver."

"Can you do anything to help me?"

"I don't want to; I want you to stop screaming and talking. That's how you get help."

"C'mon, something. This is killing me."

"I can give you a shot of steroids and it'll help you temporarily, but you gotta stop."

"Yeah, my season is over in a few weeks, after that I'll stop doing shows."

"That's not enough, the croaking whisper is worse. Just shut up. Completely."

"Yeah, thanks, give me the shot."

He did. It hurt like a bastard, but man, did that help.

I paid in cash. I don't know where my sexy-wide-open-larynx-beaver pictures ended up, but if you find them, please let me know. I walked out into the Philly streets. There was no reason for a second opinion. I was fucked. I had a lot of thinking to do. But the shot sure helped. The sore throat went away, and I could talk. I guess he was a quack, a Dr. Feelgood, who was used to working with opera cats who had to sing that night. He fixed me in the short run. I kept doing shows on weekends, though I shut up during the week.

I shut up completely when not doing shows. I wrote notes to people, like an asshole. I kept my screaming voice the same, but my talking voice started to come back, just from being quiet during the week and, of course, more steroids than Schwarzenegger. I promised myself when the season was over, I would spend a month not talking at all, and then stop screaming maybe forever. I'd already bought a sound system in cash; I would use that and work on a theater show. I'd find a new voice. This would be my last month as a street performer.

I had another living-outside-the-law-and-being-honest thing to do. I hadn't paid taxes, ever. I thought I should. I was making money, and I was living in this country, so I should pay my dues. I made an appointment with an accountant. I knew how much I was making, since I counted my money every weekend, banded my bills and rolled my change. It was my Sunday-night activity, my meditation. I'd put on a Residents record and spend a couple hours sorting, counting, and banding. It was nice and relaxing. The money was all cash. I bought everything in cash, paid all my bills in cash. If someone pissed me off, I'd pay the debt in quarters. I bought all the theater equipment in cash. I paid my rent in cash. I paid everything with my quarters and singles—if I liked the person I was paying, I went to the bank and got it changed into less-stupid money. I didn't spend the fives, tens, twenties, fifties, and hundreds, those were my savings, and I just hid them around the apartment.

People slipped drugs and phone numbers into my collection bag all the time. I told the troops to throw away the drugs. I don't know if they did, but I never saw them. If the phone numbers had a good note, or if I saw and remembered who'd dropped the note in and there was a groove, I'd give a call. During the blind-fold juggling when I was a ghost, I'd look through the gauze, and on a good night I might catch a woman I found attractive writing a note while I juggled knives wearing a pretend blindfold. I'd watch her when she didn't know she was being watched. Writing a note, she cared more about making herself known to me than watching my final trick. That was so sexy to me. And some women who I didn't see wrote great notes. I liked this one:

> *I've been here on four dates with four dif-*
> *ferent guys, and I shamed every one of them*
> *into giving you a twenty. I think you owe me*
> *dinner.*

I went out with her. We had fun.

I told the accountant how much do-re-mi I made. I couldn't work in the winter, and I only worked week-ends, but it was 1976 and I still made over 150 grand.

"If you report to the IRS that you're making that much money juggling on the street, they're going to think you're dealing drugs." He paused for effect. "*I* think you're dealing drugs."

"I'm not. I'm a good juggler."

"If it's all cash, I suggest you just shut up."

Man, I had paid a lot of money in cash for two professionals to just tell me to shut the fuck up. I had another month on the streets, and then I was going to shut the fuck up.

CHAPTER 7

It could have been my last week street performing. The quack had given me a shot of cortisone
every week for a month, and I shut the fuck up
on weekdays. I stopped drinking Chloraseptic,
so my guts started working better. I could talk
to folks after my shows on the weekends in an
almost normal voice and I didn't smell like a hospital. I'd spent a lot of jingle on the throat doc but
I still had piles of cash hidden around the house.
I told my theater group we had to get serious,
that they were going to be my only job soon. I'd
told Bee and José they had to take over Head
House. They had to find another juggler; I was
splitting.

It was getting cold at Head House. The
crowds were thinning out. Either this weekend or
the next would be our last. Soon Bee and Fats
would be done for the season, and I'd be done
forever. As it turned out, it was my last Saturday
performing on the streets. But my last Saturday

was a warm fall night—Native American summer, I guess—and we made a lot of coin. I was bummed about ending my career. I couldn't accept it. I just kept adding shows, going much later into the night than usual. I didn't want to finish for the night. I did my last show after one in the morning. It was just a little over a hundred bucks, really not worth doing. I was going out with a whimper.

Bee came up to me after the show. Since I had gone late, he'd worked late with me. He was waiting for me to finish.

"Hey man, Whopper?" Bee said.

"You feel like dining with the King?"

"Yeah."

"I'd rather go to Jim's Steaks. Let's be all Philly and shit. We gotta think in terms of the Cheez Whiz."

"You know I love Whoppers and I want to talk to you. BK is more private."

"Okay, but you're paying. You can pay with those pennies from your shows."

"You dick. Deal. We gotta talk."

"Okay, I can still kind of talk."

Bee and I walked to Burger King. It was now after two in the morning. Bee was in his cape and rhinestones, walking funky Vegas. I'd never seen him wear anything else. It was a few blocks to the BK that we favored. Bee got me the biggest Whopper with extra mayo. He got himself a normal Whopper and BK's sort of fish burger, the Whaler. He always slid the fish patty into his Whopper. He called it "surf and turf for the streets." He got us three big orders of fries to split.

A giant Coke with no ice for him and a Sprite for me. We walked upstairs to the additional dining area.

White-tile floors and walls, and fluorescent tubes blinking wicked fast. Houseflies perceive each of those blinks as long enough for a nap. Each hour was more than a human night of their fly lives flashing away before their compound eyes. People couldn't perceive the blinks consciously, but everybody got a little jumpier upstairs in the constant strobe on dirty white walls.

Some teenage BK manager was trying to throw out a couple junkies who had nodded off in his establishment. Bee led us to the front corner of the second floor, up against a window, looking out on South Street. We prepared our meals. Bee slid his fried mystery fish into his Whopper, threw away the bun, and then emptied six ketchup packs onto the wrapper for his fries. I liked ketchup but I wasn't going to work for it. I didn't want to open a zillion packets. And if I had had plenty of ketchup, I'd need a fork—I refused to lick ketchup off my fingers. I wasn't that much of a pig. I had no ketchup and no fork, so I took the limp sticks of fat and salt, considered by some to be a vegetable, and stuck them in my gob, wiping my hands on my socks, like a showbiz pro—I was wearing white pants. We were hungry. We choked down the goodness for a few minutes without speaking, just the sounds of slurping, and then Bee spoke.

"You gonna miss the streets?"

"Yeah."

"I don't think I would."

"You're wrong."

"I want out."

"What? You gonna work at a bank with a cape and glitter singing deconstructed funk?"

"Nope, ain't gonna do that. Well, maybe kinda."

I thought it was a joke that didn't land, but he was telling the truth and I missed it. "Well, you got a bunch more years, right? You can go until you're Fat Jake, blowing dogs for wine change."

"That ain't gonna happen." He took a big sloppy bite of his surf and turf. "So, no more streets for you—what are you going to do?"

"I don't know. I'm gonna try to work in theater, I guess. Do comedy and shit."

"You think you're fucking Richard Pryor?"

"Nope, not close."

There was a long pause. I kept taking breaths, leaning in to start to tell a joke or bust his balls, but every time I did, he was just too fucking serious, and I kept my mouth shut. He was about to say something heavy, so I just waited.

He looked me in the eye, like he never had. "Listen, I got an idea, a good idea, but I need a white guy who can talk."

"I can barely talk and I'm barely white. I'm carny trash and that career fucked up both those things for me."

"Fuck you, you *are* white, motherfucker, don't be an asshole. Your voice is coming back, getting stronger every day, you don't smell like Vicks VapoRub, and you got that pussy New England accent."

I had crossed some line with that "not white" thing. I understood enough why that was insensitive of me and backed down right away: "Okay." No racial/class commentary for me. I didn't know shit about that. Jesus, what was I thinking?

"Yeah, fuck you again. And I'm not talking about your voice."

Whew, we seemed to be getting past the Black/white fuckup. I got my balls back: "I do a lot of talking with my voice, retard." I'm from Massachusetts. You can't take the "retard" out of Massachusetts.

"You can talk, you always know what to say. You can think on your feet and ain't scared of shit. I seen you talk to cops, bikers, store managers, drug dealers, moms with babies, and buckets of fuck. You don't fucking care. You are always cool, and you always know what to say. And you don't look streets, man, you look like some fucking real estate asshole."

"Wait. What? No, I had hair down to my ass."

"*Used to* don't count. It's what you look like now. You look and talk like an off-the-rack white guy."

"Okay, I'm not Richard Pryor but I'm not a fucking real estate guy. Sorry, I'm a white guy who can talk and looks more like a real estate asshole than you do. We can't all be mumbling, dusky-complected, and looking like a jive slapping bass player auditioning for Parliament-Funkadelic."

"Shut up, Poe." He wasn't upset by me busting his balls, he wanted me quiet so he could get to what was on his mind. Again, he looked me right in the eye. He had to stop that shit; it creeped me out. "I got a job for us. It's all set up. I've been working weeks. It's ready to go. I just need a white guy who can talk."

"You're not talking about a street juggling/magic show, are you?"

"Nope. It's not a show." He paused. I'd never seen him scared before. "Well, I guess it is a show, an important show, but nope, it ain't showbiz. We will make millions each. Over five million each, I figure."

"Is this something that once you tell me about it, I'm an accessory before the fact, or some other TV cop bullshit? Are you Huggy Bear?"

"Stop fucking around . . ." Oops. Oh man. He was like my school principal, if Mr. Jenkins at Greenfield High had looked like James Brown and said "fuck" a lot. "You know just what the fuck I mean."

"No, I have no fucking idea what you fucking mean. I have no idea what you mean. What the fuck? What the fucking fuck? What?" I was sweating through my greasy socks.

"You do know enough about what I mean right now, and the less you know beyond that, the better off we all are."

"*All?* You said 'all,' not 'both.' Jesus."

"I told you I had some guys lined up."

"No. You didn't say that. I would have heard that. How many guys? Fuck me."

"The less you know, the better. You'll know nothing about any guys but me. All you gotta do is show your white ass and talk the way you talk, all real estate and shit, like a fucking pussy."

"I gotta show my ass? I'm down with that."

"Cut it out, Poe, before I fuck you up. This is very serious. You just need to be white and talk to some folks."

"This sounds like a really bad idea."

"It's a really *good* idea. A perfect idea. It's a lot of money. A lot. You'll never juggle anything again except some huge firm titties and your nutsack while you're fucking on a pile of money. Almost six million, Poe."

"Listen, Bee, I love you, man, I really do. Lots. But I've finished my Whopper. You can have the rest of the fries. I'm going to grab what's left of my Sprite, walk down those stairs. Tomorrow we'll do our last Sunday shows together, and this confab never happened. You know me, I forget shit. I'll forget this conversation forever. Probably be best for you if I just forget *you*. Fuck me, Bee. I love you, man, but I'm now a goofy faint memory for you, okie-doke? I was just some juggling real estate agent you saw once at Head House." I stood up, grabbed my Sprite, gave a nervous smile, and thought about how fresh and innocent the air was going to smell when I hit the safety of the Philly streets. I needed my feet and ass crack to stop sweating.

Bee grabbed my arm. It was the first time he had ever touched me. We had never even shaken hands. I'm from New England, I don't hug. But now Bee was holding my biceps hard. He was strong. Strong enough to stop time. We locked eyes. "You don't want to fuck with me, brother, trust me on this. Do not fuck with me—not on this."

CHAPTER 8

I walked into the bank scared shitless, in my real-estate-agent suit. Plastered to my sweaty upper lip was a fake porn mustache, which in the seventies was called a mustache. I wore a pretty real-looking wig, kind of a sandy blond, almost early Beatles. It felt like my sweat was soaking through it, but checking would look weird and I had to act very natural. I was wearing sunglasses and a hat—just a regular guy who happened to be sweating through his real-estate-agent shirt and tie into his real-estate-agent polyester sports jacket. There were many other people on the street who looked just like drier versions of me. Jesus, what a weird time. Everything I was wearing, even my underwear, had been bought out of town. I'd traveled 173 miles to buy all this stuff in cash—and not memorable cash, either; I'd used fifties and twenties I'd gotten out of my stash. It wouldn't do to look tall and thin on the job, so when I went to buy the real estate suit I wore padding. Padding that I was now soaking through. I'd put the padding on at home before going to the clothes store, where I tried on my suit in the dressing room. Nothing memorable about that to anyone, everyone was starting to get fat back then. Not crazy fat like now, but they were getting porky. I took a bus, no car for anyone to remember, on my shopping trip. I bought a whole set of new clothes before I left home, just to wear when I went to buy the new fat-real-estate-guy clothes. Nothing like I'd ever worn before and nothing I would ever wear again. I don't really know what this was protecting me against, but it felt like the right way to do it. It felt all criminal.

When I was a child and didn't think my clothes or my haircut were appropriate for my peer group in school, my mom would say, "Who's looking at you?" I had to make sure that was true for this. No one could be looking at me. Not even a second glance. I had to look normal, and it was tough. All I wanted to do was leave and cry.

I don't think people could see my panic. To them I was just boring and fat. I'd stuffed my cheeks like the Godfather. With Brando's cheeks stuffed, he looked like Don Vito Corleone. With mine stuffed, I looked like a chipmunk about to make an offer that couldn't be refused, and felt like a chipmunk whose teeth were chattering. But not a noticeable chipmunk. Since the night with Bee in the BK, I had been on total vocal rest, I didn't go back to the streets that next day and I really didn't say a word to anyone. Weeks of silence would alter my voice and, as a bonus, would keep me from saying anything stupid to anyone about the "job."

I didn't want to do this. I was here only because I had said yes to a Whopper. I was so scared of doing this. I have a goofy walk, but I had been practicing to not walk like that. Normally I walk like a farmer, with my feet out to the side. But I had learned to walk like a real estate agent instead of like Batman's Penguin. It wouldn't be smart to walk like a goofy fictional criminal mastermind while committing a real crime. I was walking different, I was fat, and I had no idea how my voice was going to sound when I spoke for the first time today. I had no idea if I even had a voice. I had no idea if I'd be able to talk. Can terror change a voice more than damage? Besides my complexion, I had been chosen for my ability to be calm and cool. The way I usually accomplished that was to make jokes, though I couldn't be funny for this. Funny is memorable.

Bee had picked the right guy, he really had. I believe I looked cool and calm. The more scared I was, the cooler I looked. I have that quality—a hindrance if I were drowning and calling for help, but an advantage in a bank robbery. I walked over to the desk which handled safe deposit boxes. There was a very attractive women working the desk. She introduced herself as Ms. Nathanson. No flirting, no jokes, no eye contact, give her nothing but the facts, man. She was so sexy, but I didn't have a cock, my dick had shrunk up and run to hide inside my body. Bee had given me an ID with a phony-baloney name on it.

I was carrying a driver's license for some asshole named Robert Ingersoll, yet the picture on it was me with puffy cheeks and a wig. I'd given Bee the photo and the signature, and I think he had done the forging himself. It didn't need to be perfect, just good enough to fool the sexy bank woman for an instant. She just glanced at it, then found the name in her records. Bee must have had someone rent the box with a different ID but the same name. There was no copy of the other ID in their records, I don't know why, maybe it was before Xerox was invented. Good for the crime but too bad for my imagination. I was trying to not think about dying. I tried to focus on how sexy Ms. Nathanson was, even with my dick crawling toward my pancreas. Maybe that would get me through. Don't picture life in prison, picture Ms. Nathanson's sex. I tried to forget where I was and just imagine a photocopy of Ms. Nathanson sitting naked on that copy glass with that bright light rolling under the privates, but my mind kept going back to the crime. I guess that was good. I had to know the exact time, though I couldn't keep checking my watch. I checked when I could and then counted in my head. I had to have her open the door to the vault right on schedule.

I showed Ms. PhotoBottom the box key Bee had given me and she said, "Follow me, Mr. Ingersoll." But I couldn't, not at that moment. Not yet. She couldn't open that door for me an instant before three minutes after noon. I had four minutes to kill. I've worked in improv, but no jokes and no flirting. I leaned over and tied my shoe. Brilliant. But can a fat real estate asshole tie his shoe for two hundred and eleven seconds? I tried. I then stood up slowly and fixed my tie, and adjusted my soaked asshole-real-estate jacket. Another forty-two seconds to go. I said, in my brand-new real-estate-asshole voice, "Excuse me a second (or forty-one)," surprised that my voice was clear and unwavering. It was amazing. I made a show of checking a piece of paper that I pulled out of my back pocket, and she couldn't see it was blank. I checked my watch. *Go! Go! Now! Now!* I walked quickly with her to the door. She put the key in the lock. Timing seemed right.

And it was! Right as she opened the door, I heard terrified screaming coming from the front of the bank. We both froze. A guy with a gun came running up and roughly pushed Ms. AssOnGlass out of the way. I was relieved beyond words. My part was almost over. He stuck the gun to my head and said, "Gimme all the fucking keeeys, man! Now!" Wait, was this Bee in a ski mask with a lousy Mexican accent? Like the chivalrous real estate asshole I was, I gave him my single box key and pointed to Ms. PhotoBottom, whose attractive bottom was likely now dripping piss. Her turn to be scared shitless (kind of mixing clichés, but not really).

Señor Bee, or whoever the fuck he was, put the gun on her and she gave him every key she had, probably including the key to her junior high Hello Kitty diary.

"Which one's the vault?"

She showed him. He took all the keys and started

moving. I figured later that the Ingersoll safety deposit box (I'll do both "safe deposit" and "safety deposit" so I have more of a chance of being right and a certainty of being wrong) must have been filled with copies to all the keys for the other boxes in the vault. At the time banks kept copies of everyone's private key (this was outlawed a few years later, probably because of this event), and some disgruntled employee had sold all those copies to Bee (I bet he paid in quarters). Whoever had rented the Ingersoll box had put them all in the one box. Having the keys to all the boxes was probably the only plan Bee had. When he said the job was "all set up," what he meant was he had bought a lot of keys. What a putz.

I've thought about this a lot. I've thought about it every day of my life since. I guess the plan was to take the key to the box that I had given him, and Ms. PussyBrite's key, and open the box with all the keys and use those keys and the bank keys to open all the boxes and steal all that shit. I guess Bee had a fence (does it turn you on when I talk all criminal?) that could move wills, deeds, military medals, and blackmail pictures of people's bosses, along with some pearls and diamonds, for long green. Fucking idiot.

He yelled at me: "Get the fuck out of here!" He was still doing a racist Frito Bandito kind of accent. I ran to the front. While the safe deposit boxes were being looted, and the rest of the gang was getting whatever cash they could from the tellers and hostages, I was supposed to join the other hostages and run out of the bank. This was the last part of my role. All I wanted was to run. My panic had turned to claustrophobia. The bank felt like it was shrinking and had no air. I had to get the fuck out now. My last move was to run to the door. The plan was that one of the other accomplices, who weren't white guys and couldn't talk but had guns, would yell "Stop!" like José Jiménez—and when I didn't stop, he'd shoot over my head. I was part of a magic act like some Vegas magician freak. I'd have a gun shot at me and not be hurt. So fucking stupid. But this part of the idiotic plan worked. They yelled stop, or whatever the Spanglish equivalent was, and I kept running out the door. I heard the gun fire and was so glad I had already planned to throw these pants away. Fucking loud and terrifying. But I heard it, heard it hit metal, so they'd missed as planned. Just like movies, with time slowed down by my fear, I heard the shot ricochet, and I heard more screaming. It sounded horrible, but all I knew was that I was outside. I could breathe, I could move.

When I hit the streets, people were just starting to react to the shot and gather around. They weren't organized enough to be able to tell I was leaving the bank. I kept my head down and walked like a normal real estate asshole away from the bank.

I had stashed my hippie clothes under a dumpster in an alley a block away. I stripped off the wig, the mustache, and all my clothes, and put them in a trash bag. I was standing naked for a few moments. I'd left a towel there because I had predicted my flop-sweat. There was a lot more than that in my clothes.

I toweled off and put the towel in the trash bag, with all the clothes, the hat, the fat suit, the wig, and the mustache. This was before the use of DNA evidence. If it had been a thing then, my clothes lacked only one bodily fluid. If I had taken a moment to cum in my pants about Ms. Nathanson riding the copy machine, they would have had a full set. In my stash I had bell-bottom jeans, a tie-dyed Dead shirt, a headband (although my hair wasn't that long), and beat-up sneakers. I threw away the sunglasses and put on my granny glasses. I put the trash bag with the shitty real estate clothes into my hippie knapsack and walked out of the alley. My fashion was about six years behind the real hippies, but there were still losers who looked like me. Yet none of them was as big a loser as I was right now.

CHAPTER 9

'd gotten to the nearest bus stop and taken the next bus to the end of the line. I didn't know where the fuck I was, and I hoped that meant that no one else knew where the fuck I was. I found the nearest commercial dumpster to that bus stop and casually threw in my big pissy trash bag.

I walked in a random direction until I found another bus stop and waited for the next bus to nowhere. I sat on the bus with Dustin Hoffman's lost smile at the end of *The Graduate*. In four days I was to meet Bee—or whoever he decided to send—but I would never know the rest of "my" crew. I'd make the meeting and get my share of the money, the millions I was going to convert to a big pile of cash to fuck on for the rest of my life.

I took the next bus to the end of the line and walked until I found an appliance store with a TV in the window, and stopped to see if there was news. It was almost three o'clock.

I was nobody. Just a stupid hippie, ten years too late, like all the hippies. The 1960s happened in the seventies. I stood there on the street. I looked at the TV for just a few minutes, and then my whole body jerked back. Suddenly cold and sweaty, I almost passed out. There was no sound on the TV, and no closed caption, but the news was breaking so there was a chyron. The female newscaster was looking very grave and the bottom third of the screen read: "Mother of three shot dead in bank shooting."

I think I died at that moment. The ricochet that I heard. The shot had gone over my head, caromed off of a beam, and hit a mother. We had killed a mother. I had been a murderer for almost three hours before I knew it. I couldn't hear the fucking TV. I was a murderer. That's not all I knew from the TV; it was all I knew in the world. I didn't know my name. I didn't really know how to stand up. I leaned against the window glass.

Standing seemed impossible, but somehow I walked away from the store. I found a bench at the bus stop and I fell onto it. It took all my muscles to wiggle out of my pack and put it on the bench beside me. I had been prepared for Bee's job going sideways. *Job?* It wasn't a fucking job; it was a murder, and I was part of it. I had previously thought that felony murder was kind of bullshit. Why should you be guilty of a murder if you didn't have a weapon, if you weren't even at the scene? If you just sat outside in the car or talked to a Xerox-ass woman. Now my heart knew that felony murder was true like ice like fire minus zero no limit. My heart knew that I was part of killing that woman. I wanted to confess. I wanted to go to the nearest police station and say I'd been the front man for the crew. My body instead decided to sleep on it. I was no part of the decision, but I was sleeping right there, on a bench.

Just a hippie with his head resting on a dirty knapsack. In that knapsack was a toothbrush, toothpaste, some deodorant (I wasn't a perfect hippie), a bottle of aspirin, two pairs of fresh underwear (I was a terrible hippie), two pairs of socks, a clean Alice Cooper *Love It to Death* T-shirt, a Mickey Mouse T-shirt in DayGlo psychedelic colors, a pair of cutoff jeans, and eighty-seven thousand dollars in cash. That wasn't all the money I'd ever made on the streets—it was the fives, tens, twenties, fifties, and hundreds. I'd made almost that amount again in ones and change. I'd spent a lot of that, and the rest I'd left in a closet in my apartment.

I slept a little, my head bent over, drooling, like in an institution for people who sleep sitting up and drooling. I woke up just enough to reach into the pack, reach through the money, and find my aspirin. I took eight tablets. I think I read somewhere that aspirin helps emotional pain too. Probably bullshit. I probably needed Bayer heroin (which was the company's first product), but I took them one by one and swallowed them without water. It felt right that the bitterness stuck in my dry throat. I rested my head on everything I had in the world and fell asleep. A couple hours later a nice policeman woke me up: "Hey, kid, you can't sleep here, you gotta get moving."

"Sorry, sir."

"Just take your stuff and get off the bench."

"Sorry. What time is it?"

"It's a bit before five."

"Okay, I just need a minute."

"Hurry up," and he was on his way. I reached into my pack and pulled out a few fives and a couple twenties, put them in the pocket of my jeans, and headed to a bar for the first time in my life. It had a TV over the bar and they weren't playing sports. I put my pack at my feet and ordered a ginger ale. I gave the bartender a five so he wouldn't throw me out for not drinking. The sound was up on the TV and the news was coming on. The lead story was the bank robbery. The felony-murderer bank robbers had gotten away. One hostage had been shot dead, a young mother. Another would-be hostage had run out of the bank and couldn't be found (that was me). They had been technically hostages, but not for long—the criminals had left when they got the money, so in the end they had just been casual hostages. The Philly police were looking for five Mexican American men; the Frito Bandito accents had worked. They weren't looking for African American men and they weren't looking for me.

They'd gotten away with all the money from the tellers, though the reporter didn't say how much that was, so I couldn't figure out what my share would be. There was no mention of the deposit box vault, so either that part failed or the bank didn't want it known. Most likely it just failed. Bee and the guys probably got less money than I had in my knapsack, and we'd killed a woman for it.

The newscast moved on to born-again Jimmy Carter. I finished crunching the ice in my glass and asked the bartender for some matches. I went to an alley at the end of the block and found a patch of street with nothing else around. I took my driver's license, and I lit it on fire. It's harder to do that than I thought, but after a couple tiny burns to my fingers, I got it all burned. I looked around, whipped out my dick, and pissed on the smoldering ashes of my identity. No more Poe.

I wasn't going to the meeting Bee had set up. I wasn't going to meet anyone. I wasn't going back to my apartment. I wasn't going to call my theater partners. The world would be without the new half-assed Richard Pryor. The hot dog woman, Tracy, had become a pretty steady girlfriend and had been sleeping at my apartment all the time. She had keys. The rent was paid including the last month and my security deposit. I hoped she'd get some use out of it. I hoped she'd open the closet and take all the singles and quarters and bring them to the bank. I was never going to call her again. I left her with about thirty grand and my hitchhiking herpes to remember me by.

My parents had died the year before, which was probably part of the reason I'd done this stupid thing anyway. My sister had married a born-again preacher and moved into some church/cult/commune. No one would ever hear from me again. No one. I'd be missed, though just a little.

I took some more money out of my pack and started walking to the Philly train station. It was a long walk, but I needed a long walk. I needed to wander my scorched earth. I had just killed a woman. The walk wasn't going to clear my head, that was for sure, and there was nothing to think about. Nothing I could fix. I didn't think, I just walked. I kept walking. I got to the train station after nine at night. I looked at the board, yet I couldn't focus enough to read it. I don't know how long I stood blinking, hearing the flip cards flip. When I could finally focus, I saw a train leaving in ten minutes. I went up to the booth: "Does that train, the *North Coast Hiawatha* (I bet that name was changed soon after), go all the way to Saint Paul, Minnesota in one run?"

"If you mean you don't have to change trains? Yes. But it stops."

"When does it get in?"

"Friday at eight a.m."

"Wow, that's a long time."

"Thirty-six hours and twenty-seven minutes. Almost a thousand miles."

"Is there any sort of sleeper car, or don't they do that anymore?"

"There's just premium. You can sleep in your seat."

I could sleep sitting up and drooling like in that imaginary institution where I belonged. Damn, I had been hoping for a real sleeper car like the Three Stooges slept in, looking forward to making that *meep meep meep* sleeping sound that Shemp made when he slept.

I bought a premium ticket in cash and got on the train with my two changes of clothes and an astonishing amount of cash. It was like I had robbed a bank. I *had* robbed a bank, but this money was from juggling on the streets. Fuck me. As far as I could figure, no one was looking for me. And wouldn't be for quite a while. If Bee and his guys got away, well, the police wouldn't ever be looking for me, except as a hostage who vanished. Who cares? They wouldn't even know a white guy was part of the crew, they'd just keep harassing Mexican Americans. Police business as usual.

Most likely Bee would get caught. He would give me up right away. Tell the police they had a white guy. He'd give the police my name. They'd find my address, but I was gone. Go ahead, talk to my girlfriend, talk to my theater troupe, talk to everyone I ever met. They didn't know where I was. Fuck, *I* didn't know where I was. It was the middle of the night, and I was warm and safe and might as well have been on my way to Sortie or the Minnesota equivalent. I couldn't go to Canada, I'd burned and pissed on my ID. But Saint Paul was far up there. I decided I'd go to its twin, Minneapolis, and maybe go to Hibbing, birthplace of Bob Dylan and home of the world's largest open-pit iron mine.

Even now, forty-eight years later, you can still find a place to buy most anything in cash, but back then it was super easy. I'd be okay for a long time without an ID, though I'd need one eventually.

CHAPTER 10

I walked the streets that Bob Dylan had walked just eighteen years before. I checked into the Androy Hotel. It had been a luxury establishment way before Bob was born. All the fancy-schmancy guests of the mining company stayed there. Now it was a run-down ghost hotel. It would be bankrupt in a few months, so I was able to check in without any ID. They were just happy to see some cash to hide from the creditors.

I had had plenty of time on the train to think about what my new name should be, but I didn't. It's so odd that I also didn't think about the murder. There was nothing in my brain about it—yet my whole body had changed. The murder was now part of who I was. In my heart, guilt, shame, and regret were part of who I was, part of my name. It was so far beyond shame, even beyond guilt and regret, even beyond self-loathing. I was different. Something I had never felt before was now a big part of who I was. I didn't think about any of this on the train ride. I felt it, but I didn't think about anything, I just watched America speed by, all the poor backyard clotheslines and factory parking lots. All the gray. Over the day and a half, I tried everything on their "Peanut Special" menu in honor of Jimmy Carter. I don't know how I slept, but I slept. I slept a lot. I was kind of in a weird state of half sleep the whole time. It wasn't like my unconscious had a lot of work to do—all of me knew I was a murderer. I considered living on the train until I got thrown off for having just three filthy shirts and no shower.

I arrived. Fuck Minneapolis. I got a bus right from Saint Paul to Hibbing. No ID needed.

I was in Hibbing, and I had to create my new identity. I couldn't use Zimmerman—there were other Zimmermans in this town and that might fuck me up. I don't look like a Zimmerman, neither Dylan nor Deadmau5. I loved the Residents like I loved Dylan. They were an anonymous avant-garde band out of San Francisco. They were on Ralph Records and managed by the Cryptic Corporation. If you read all their album jackets carefully, and I did, you'd find that one of the people who worked there was named Hardy Fox, and he was called "H." What if I just stole his name and his nickname? He worked for an anonymous band, what would he care? I wasn't going to steal his identity or his credit rating, just use his name.

Too stupid. Hardy Fox is memorable, and memorable was a bad idea for me. The most common name in the world is Mohammad, but I look less like a

Mohammad than a Zimmerman. The most common name in the USA is Michael Jackson. Mike Jackson was perfect. Wait, my new imaginary parents would want to be a tiny bit original. I'd be Mick Jackson. Mick Jackson, that's me. But I'd always wanted to be known almost exclusively by a nickname. How about Tiny, a tiny bit original. I was six foot seven, so that would work ironically, and I loved Tiny Tim. Perfect. A guy my size being called Tiny is memorable? Is that a problem? I guess it would be better to be Mick to everyone, but I needed some personality. The police weren't looking for a big guy named Tiny, so fuck it, I couldn't be completely beige—I wanted to be Tiny.

I needed to start working on being officially Mick; Tiny would take care of himself. I went to the Hibbing library and got a card in the name of Mick Jackson. "Hey, I know a Mike Jackson," said the librarian who would be beautiful without her glasses and was even more beautiful with them. I guess I was going to get comments like that a lot. I liked it.

I took a deep breath and tried out, "People call me Tiny."

She smiled. "Hello, Tiny." I liked my name on her lips. I was Tiny.

She said her name was Marion. I said, "I'm not singing 'Marion the Librarian' to you." Jesus, I guess Tiny was comedically a hack, though she didn't roll her eyes. She giggled a little and I liked that even more. I started wondering if the library had a copy machine. No, not to copy Marion the librarian's cunt, get your mind out of the gutter. I thought maybe I could do some forgery with a copy machine, using Liquid Paper (thanks to Mike Nesmith's mom).

Marion showed me where I could find information on Minnesota forms and records. I needed more help, yet I couldn't have Marion know what I was doing. Without her, finding exactly what I needed would be slow, but I had time. I waited until she'd gone to the desk to help another patron, and I clumsily found what I needed. Minnesota had pictures on their driver's licenses, fuck. But North Dakota didn't. North Dakota barely had running water. All this information was right there. Even copies of what the ND licenses looked like. Before my body had turned to carrion, Marion the librarian came back and I asked her to show me the copy machine and loan me some Liquid Paper. I kept wanting to lie to her about what I was doing, but she never asked. Librarian/client privilege? The first thing you learn about lying is don't answer questions that aren't asked. Don't run when no one is chasing you. She didn't care, so I worked on. Goddamn, libraries have everything for the felony-murder hippie who never wants to be an ex-con.

I photocopied a North Dakota driver's license out of the book. I used Liquid Paper (the real brand was Wite-Out, but I wanted to thank Nez's mother, so I lied, sorry). I resized it on the copy machine. Marion let me use her typewriter and I typed my name, *Mick Jackson*, on the clean copy of the form. She just showed me the typewriter and went on stacking books. I took a moment to enjoy her body's standing waves. Jesus, the books weren't the only things that were stacked. I went back to work. I looked at a few library maps of ND and found an address I liked. I made Tiny's birthday a year and a few months earlier than the old one. Why not? Aquarius is a good bullshit sign for a bullshit hippie. Yeah, I needed corrective lenses, I'd check that box. Might as well be honest about my eyes on my forgery. I photocopied all that again and used Marion's scissors to cut it out. I now had a kinda ND driver's license. If you commit a horrible crime and want help getting away with it, go to the library. They have all the tools.

With my bullshit ND driver's license, I went and found an apartment. I gave the landlord first and last month's rent and the deposit, all in cash, and the slack asshole didn't even look at my fake driver's license. He should have been careful—he might have rented an apartment to a felony murderer. I walked around the town and tried to find a store where I could sign up to have them send stuff in my name to my address. I needed to establish Tiny Mick Jackson in the world.

It was too cold to juggle outside, and my apartment had low ceilings, and I really needed to juggle. It was too dangerous to perform in public, yet I needed that meditative manipulation of objects. I joined the YMCA using my ND driver's license, my library card, and cash. I had them send my YMCA membership card to my new address. The YMCA was run by a Jack LaLanne kind of cat. A push-ups guy, very clean-cut. When he finished filling out all my membership stuff, I 'fessed up—not to being a felony murderer, but to being a juggler. I asked him if, during times when they weren't busy, I could stand over in the corner of the gym on a few mats and practice juggling. He said sure. He said that they had "Indian clubs" at the Y that I could use.

Jesus christ, how fucking stupid can you fucking get? Idiot. It's like saying that jugglers use bowling pins to juggle. He was a nice guy, but the asshole knew dick about juggling. He was thrilled to have a Young Man Christian juggler to Associate with. But I needed proper clubs to practice. There was no juggling store in Hibbing, or anyplace else in the world, and the guys who made juggling stuff that I could send away for would need a check, and Tiny was several weeks away from getting a checking account. I went to the hardware store (I so wanted to buy an appliance at Zimmerman's—Bob's dad and uncle—but my apartment came with all that appliance shit already). I bought a couple of brooms, a saw, some colorful tape, glue, and a sharp razor knife. I was lucky the quaint little toy store had just the right rubber balls so I could make the kind of juggling props I'd used when hitchhiking. I cut my broomsticks to the right length, carved a hole in each rubber ball, glued them on, and now had juggling clubs that would feel right for practice, and have at least a little color on them—although juggling is as much tactile as visual. Juggling blindfolded was always part of my act; although it was fake, and mostly just an excuse to look at women, I'd always felt I could actually do it. I *could* do it; I just chose not to. I'm kind of like those "psychics" who convince themselves that they can really read minds and predict the future, but just to be safe, why not switch the papers and force the numbers?

The Amazing Randi was a big hero of mine. I met him once under my felony-murderer name, my dead name, but could I meet him as Tiny? He wouldn't remember, he meets a lot of people. I decided to write Randi a fan letter and ask for an autographed picture, *To Tiny*, and have it sent to Mick Jackson's address. I could use that envelope at the DMV. I'm a genius, and you should be skeptical of that.

CHAPTER 11

I visited the Y every day to work on my four and five clubs. I also went to the library every day; I love to read and sometimes Marion would bend over to rectify the lower shelves. I apologize, maybe you were right to assume I'd be thinking about her ass on a copy machine. I often had a sandwich at the Y, but I was thinking more and more about eating at Marion's Y.

I want to write more stupid jokes about eating pussy. Why the fuck was the TV show *Petticoat Junction* never busted for "petticoat junction" just meaning the pussy at the junction of the legs under the petticoat? I guess the decency leagues were napping on *Petticoat Junction*, Beaver Cleaver, and Hogan's Hero. (I just threw in the last one to fuck you up—I don't think there was anything offensive about that show other than laughing about death camps.)

Marion and I were flirting more and more, soon I was going to ask her out. I felt I had a chance. I was at the library a lot and I never saw any guy or gal come in to pick her up. So far, Marion and the Jack LaLanne guy at the Y were the only people to call me Tiny, because they were the only people I talked to, but I liked it. I was starting to feel like Tiny. I wasn't just pretending to be another person; I was *becoming* another person, a new person born again in real original sin. Way back in the alley by the bank, right after the robbery, I had pulled off my fake mustache and I hadn't shaved since then. I now had a light beard. My mom said it was because I was part Native American. I hope you believe that—I don't want you thinking it's a lack of ball power. I had been over a month without shaving and I was getting that baby-hippie, Bob's *Nashville Skyline* fuzz. *Fuzz-faced* is what Tiny looked like. I had gone shopping and besides buying underwear and socks (I needed them badly, but we needn't go into that), I bought flannel shirts and jeans. I bought jeans that were for working and not for bell-bottoming. It was that kind of hippie I wanted to be, and I wanted Marion to be partial to.

I didn't want to ask Marion out before I had a driver's license. No, not because of "Bend over, I'm driving, baby," you pig, but rather because if I got busted at the DMV, my heart would be less broken when I had to leave Marion forever without another word.

I wanted to know Marion better, so I had to go to the DMV. If I pulled this off, I would have an ID. A passport was a long way off, and I still wouldn't have a Social Security number, but I didn't need one for a license—and a driver's license will get you a long way. I guess what I should have done was found a dead child and taken their name and Social, but being Mick Jackson without a Social was okay with me. I was never going to have a straight job. I hadn't changed that much.

The DMV in Hibbing is very Hooterville (wait, that's also from *Petticoat Junction*, was that show nothing but tits and ass?). A DMV very different from Philly, and that's good and bad for felony forgery. The person working the desk had seen me around. I told them I'd moved from North Dakota, and it was time to make the move official. He asked me, "Whereabouts?" Oops. I had walked up to a person who knew something about North Dakota. What are the odds? Well, in Hibbing, pretty good, but I had prepared a little. I'd picked my ND town for my fake address, and I had read a little bit about it.

"Like it says on my license, I was in Minot, a little outside of Minot actually. I was doing some work for MSU. Do you know Minot?"

"Well, I know Ward County, but for my people, Minot's too big of a city."

"Well, Minot is not NYC, but I thought Hibbing was even more my speed."

"What are you doing here in Hibbing?"

"Well, I had some money saved for the move, and now I want to just get my bearings for a while."

"Yeah, well, it's a good little town, Mick."

"You can call me Tiny."

This was the funniest thing Mr. DMV had ever

heard. Well, slap my ass and call me Sally. He couldn't get over it. "Tiny? Tiny!? What are you, six foot four or something?"

"A few inches taller than that, actually."

"And folks call you Tiny. Well, doesn't that just beat everything? My wife isn't going to believe this."

"Well, maybe if you lied to her less, she would believe you." Oops. Fuck. I thought this would be cute and funny, but it wasn't playing in the Hibbing DMV.

"What?"

I ignored his question and what I had said to prompt it. "Well, you can tell her that I got the nickname when I was a baby, and I was tiny, but the truth is it happened in junior high when I was even taller than all the girls." I was going to add, *and I had bigger tits too*, but I was learning about my audience and adjusting my material.

"Tiny. Tiny. I can't wait to tell Cindy. Tiny. Tiny. Tiny." He was just muttering my name like a comedy mantra, but he was also filling out all the paperwork. Thank you, Tiny.

He simply couldn't get over it, he liked my name more than I liked my first blowjob (both giving and receiving, so I guess my first *two* blowjobs). He grinned all over, "So . . . *Tiny* . . . let's get your picture, huh?"

I stood in front of the camera looking as much like Mick Jackson as I could and feeling like Tiny. He snapped it and said, "We got to get this processed, so here's your temp license without the picture and we'll mail you the real license in a few days. You don't have to come in again, Tiny."

And that was it. A few pieces of mail to my apartment in my name, a library card, and my forged ND driver's license, and here I was: Tiny Jackson. Damn.

With my temporary license, I could at least ask Marion out to lunch. She accepted without hesitation. We sat over grilled cheese, potato chips, and a half pickle each, and for the first time in my life I did well on a date. I was good. Tiny's dating advice: don't be you. It's so simple. All the stupid stories I always told about my life, those weren't my life anymore, I couldn't tell them. My stories about hopping trains and street performing, all those stories I wrote down for you, most of this book so far, I couldn't tell Marion any of them, because none of them happened to Tiny. I had no boring glory-days stories of Tiny's to tell, so instead I listened to her. It seemed like no man in her life had ever done that. I would have never done that if I were still me. I couldn't be distracted thinking about what I was going to say next, because I had nothing to say next. I didn't think about how I was going to lead into my brilliant story about fucking over the string quartet in New Market because that wasn't Tiny's story, and it wasn't that brilliant.

I was ready to listen. I wasn't going to be impatient with her life and her hopes and dreams. Nothing she said was going to be boring. I would listen. Not thinking about what I was going to say next, and how I was going to impress her, allowed me to think about another human being who wasn't me. I was listening to her and loving it. Probably just because of that, she looked like she was loving *me*. Mick Jackson's how-to-pick-up-chicks: Do not be yourself. Listen.

And it turned out Marion was worth listening to.

CHAPTER 12

Yes, she was very worth listening to. She had a story to tell.

"I didn't go to college for library science. I went to the University of Minnesota with the dream of being a dentist. They have a good dentistry school. The world looks at me and thinks, *That is the body of a dental hygienist—*"

"I was thinking just that."

"—but I wanted to be a dentist. I wanted to have a career with a high suicide rate, and I didn't have enough talent to be in the arts. That's not true. Neither part is true. I have enough talent to be a talentless artist, and it's a myth about suicide and dentists. Highest suicide rates are construction workers, miners, and hunters. Hunters killing themselves makes me laugh. It means there's a lot of time for dangerous self-reflection in the forest, *I can't outsmart an ungulate? Oh, the shame! Well, my firestick is right here . . . Forensics will think a white-tailed deer took me out and my family will still get the insurance money.* Yeah, I was treated very badly in dental school."

"I'm sorry."

"Thank you. *Very* badly, let's just say *Ms.* mag missed them by a macho mile, and I wouldn't let them win by falling back to hygienist. Undergrad wasn't any problem; I got my bachelor's and all the credits. I even made it through three of the four years of dental college, and then some bad things happened. Several. It wasn't worth it anymore. I was getting to hate people—not people: men. And I enjoy liking men, so I transferred to library science. Much more enlightened.

"During all my time at college I went often to the Dudley Riggs Brave New Workshop and saw a lot of live improv comedy. I loved it. I was in the big city, and for a farm girl like me, that seemed so sophisticated and far out. Men in comedy treated me with more respect than wannabe dentists, and that is damning with faint praise. I took a few classes at the workshop and even did a few shows."

"You did comedy?"

"Yeah, even with the body of a dental hygienist. I wasn't terrible. I was funny now and again, and not just 'yes and' sex jokes. I was okay. Some of my jokes moved to the weekend shows, but someone else performed them. I didn't like being onstage. I seriously considered directing for a while. I think I have an eye and the taste, but to be a director you need to be the kind of person who thinks she can cut her own hair. You need to have a pathological faith in your own skills. I don't have that, and I don't like telling people what to do. To direct, you have to love telling people what to do.

"I saw Al Franken at the Brave New Workshop a couple of times with Tom Davis, and both were way more enlightened than dentists in training. I saw Franken and Davis before *SNL*, and we all hung out a bit. I'm older than you. I saw the year on your driver's license when you oddly bragged about it and waved it in my face."

"That was a little weird, wasn't it?"

"Yeah, but not without charm. It was during my improv time that I had a very intense, profound, and bothersome experience. One of the guys at the workshop, he had some of your charm, wanted to be a professional skeptic or something. One of those atheist-as-a-career types. Hey, buddy, we all know there's no god, how about you open a comic book shop and shut up? But he was cute, and we were hanging out a lot. Have you heard of the Amazing Randi?"

"Yes, I've met him."

"I figured. I guess I have a type. It seemed like my guy, why don't I use his name? James. Not Jim, James. James wanted to set up some skeptic stings, like Randi. He wanted to video himself doing all these scams. He had one of the first highfalutin Betamax cameras. He was making a demo tape for a show he wanted to sell to TV. He wanted to make it in Minnesota, sell it in LA, and then go national. His plan was to use his show to eliminate all the bullshit in the world."

"Seems he was successful."

"Totally. He had shot a few of the segments and they weren't bad. I wrote a few of the jokes, but girlfriends aren't credited, fucking dentists. He did his how-to segment with Geller spoon-bending that was very funny. Remember Geller?"

"Asshole."

"That's him. Well, James was teaching spoon-bending in one video and that was in the can. It was funny. He wanted another segment on cryptozoology, so I was researching Chupacabra for him. It means 'goat sucker.'"

"What did you call me?"

"You heard me. I loved doing the research. It was my library sciences soul tugging at my sleeve. The big scam of James's show, the centerpiece, was going to be a hidden-camera thing on fortune-telling, astrology, palmistry, or tarot. Doesn't matter, they're just different flavors of the same shit. They all use cold reading. I was learning a lot about it. You know cold reading?"

"Yup. From Randi."

"Sure. Well, I read a lot about it. And I put the information together for 'James not Jim.' I had encapsulated the basic rules of thumb from the several books and many articles I'd found. I had a cheat sheet of all the key points, and I started trying to work with him on it. I had no experience, but I had a feel for it right away. I understood the basic trick, but I wanted to know the culture it was built on. The beliefs it preyed upon. There were books I needed to read that weren't in the library or any real bookstore, so off I went to the college-town, hippie-Zen, new-age store to buy some books. Goodness gracious. It was tough. I've gone into a sex shop and bought an industrial alternating-current, plug-in vibrator with no real embarrassment, just a pleasurable naughty blush. There was a defiant pride, I enjoyed that purchase."

"Can we talk more about that?"

"Maybe later. I'm telling you a story now. An important story that changed me. It kind of made me who I am now. When I went into this new-age store, one of the BNW guys pronounced it *newage*, to rhyme with *sewage*. Seems right. I felt humiliated in that store, and not the good flush-blush kind of embarrassment. There was so much wrong with just walking in there. Even though no one knew me, I didn't want anyone to think I believed that shit. That was mortifying, and I was also uncomfortable with my disrespect for people who honestly believed."

"But they were wrong to believe that shit."

"Of course they were wrong, but that's not the point. My presence was mocking. My very presence had a smug cruelty that, even though they couldn't perceive it, was in my heart. I could feel it and I didn't like it. I wasn't a credulous idiot like the other people in there, but in seeing them as idiots and not wanting to be seen with them, I could no longer see myself as kind. My self-image had always included kind. But in that store, I looked like a credulous idiot and felt like a hateful cynic. My whole body knew it was wrong. It was a warmth in my face and chest that signaled no joy. I had to go home and take a shower . . . and before you say a word, we will talk about that later too.

"I brought the books home and read them. I picked up the vocabulary, and the rhythm of the thinking. Next, I had to work with James and get him to where I was so he could pull the scam for his TV show. I told him he needed to start the reading with the right inflection, and I gave him a 'graph to learn. He didn't memorize it but he kind of got the gist. I told him after he did that opening, he had to listen and listen hard. He had to be comfortable with a little silence. This wasn't stand-up, it wasn't the morning radio that he'd done. He had to wait quietly for them to tell him everything. Then he would tell them the same stuff right back with a spooky twist. We practiced, with me playing the mark, and he wouldn't let me talk. That's when I started to realize that maybe he was a dick. He couldn't even listen to me to practice for a gag.

"The psychic's real job is all the stuff James didn't do: eye contact, a gentle smile, nodding when someone else was talking. All he had to do was listen, nod like it was all already in the cards, and paraphrase it. When you get the groove, try a few guesses. When you're wrong, either ignore it, or twist it, push it, and change it until it seems like you are right. It's all finesse. And oh my goodness, James had no finesse. None. I played the pigeon, and he played the psychic. He was a steamroller, a tank. He couldn't even listen to me telling him to listen to other people. You can't do didactic fortune-telling. He sucked. He wanted the focus to be on him, but all the focus must be on the victim. That's the way the trick works. To be a fortune-telling star, you must be able to listen before you swoop in and take all the credit.

"He didn't even listen to me about how badly he sucked; he thought he was great. I got him set up at a party in Dinkytown so he could try it under fire for actual punters before he did the real taping. I did all I could for him. I picked out his clothes, got him a tarot deck, and wrote a few jokes to break the ice before the speech he hadn't really learned. I'm making him sound like such a dick. Well, he was enough of a dick for me to break up with him, but he had a lot of good qualities that don't happen to be covered in this story."

"Let's save his good points for a later time."

"We went to the party together. I found him the marks and prepped them. By the time they sat down, before James even walked into the room, I had them believing. It took him less than ten minutes to blow the whole thing. He was arguing with people about their own lives."

"He sure sounds like a dick."

"See? I have a type. The sign we had outside the room said, *Tarot by Lenny*. He picked that because he was a big Lenny Bruce fan."

"I love Lenny Bruce."

"Yup, the type. I took over the psychic role to show him how it was done. He would stay in the room like he was my handler, shut up, and watch. Women with men's names are cute, so I was Miss Lenny. Even with all my research and practice, even with my time onstage, I was so nervous. I had put James in the closest thing he had to a flamboyant suit—men are easy to dress. I was his handler, now miraculously psychic herself. I was dressed in a flowing low-cut purple gown that featured my pair of talents. It's neither feminist nor librarian of me, but I love featuring cleavage and I love wearing makeup. I looked like an eccentric hussy in touch with her feelings. I looked like a sensitive woman. In the time after James failed and before my first reading, I walked around for a while with James's tarot cards in my hand going over the lines I had tried to teach him and recalling all the crib notes I had prepared and he had ignored.

"James was better at setting me up than he was closing the deal. The first person he brought in for me, I owned. Completely. It was so natural for me. So easy. Yes, I had read all the books, but I also had a natural talent. I like listening to people. I like attempting to understand what they're trying to say. My heart seeks the truth people lay out between the lines."

"Like when I asked you out for a grilled cheese?"

"That wasn't subtext, Tiny, that was text. I fanned out my cards and I was all-knowing. I went into my spiel while I was looking her up and down. My opening spiel made her want to help and gave me an out when I was wrong: 'The cards tell me a story. I receive pictures and images that will not mean anything to me, but perhaps are very significant to you. If you remain open, we can explore together and find insights into your destiny.' Then I launched into the usual statements that appeal to everyone. Whenever I was in doubt, I just said things that I would want to be true about myself. She was into it. I stared at her and for some reason, all of a sudden, she looked like a nurse to me. I asked if she was a healer. 'Healer' gave me outs. She had certainly nurtured somebody, but I didn't need any outs. As I was saying 'healer,' I saw her face and added, right away, before she said it, 'a nurse.' Sometimes X equals X and nurses look like nurses. I can't articulate what cues I picked up, but a lucky guess is a major hit. I was golden. I was rolling the rest of the night. The standard stuff would hook them and then I would start making guesses based on my observations and their feedback. I watched them closely. I listened. I paid attention to each person like they were the only person in the world. I started to understand that the scam was not about pretending to predict the future, the scam was *listening* to people. It's all people want and so few relationships deliver that.

"All my research, acting, and improv were paying off and I was getting good, fast. *Too* good. I started out being okay and by the end of my first night I had a woman cry on me. To the motherfuckers that really do this, that's just money, but to me, well, it was awful. Then she went away sobbing, and I was broken. I had meddled in her life. She had learned nothing real about herself or her situation, but I found out a lot about myself. When James and I were alone in the room after she left, he smiled ear to ear. He had watched me reduce a woman to tears, and his first thought was, *This will be great television*."

"Wow."

"I was shook but I kept going. I tried to end all the readings with bromides like, 'You have good instincts. Trust yourself. You make your own magic.' These were words that at least alluded to self-responsibility. It was shocking how easy it was to suck people in. I had done a week of research and people believed I could 'see.' I was freaked. James was no help, he had stardust in his eyes. I had to keep taking breaks from readings and from James to just sit alone and try to feel like a good person.

"I didn't need a week of study; I can teach you everything right now. People want to feel listened to and hear positive things about themselves. That's all it is. Listen and tell them what they want to hear. Make some guesses and keep going when you miss. And I had some big misses. I turned over a card with a queen who has a cat seated at her feet, so I thought, *What the heck*: 'Do you have a cat?' The woman replied, 'No.' 'Does a friend, or someone you know, have a cat?' 'No.' What are the chances of that? But I took a break and soldiered on. 'Okay,' I said, 'keep that,' then dropped it and hit another line of bullshit. At the end of the reading, I smugly stated, 'In two weeks, when that cat shows up, you think of me, okay?' I didn't have to win right then; I could win in two weeks. You know, if a cat showed up a decade later, I would win. It's so easy, it's heartbreaking."

"Wow. Holy shit. Wow."

"Yeah, that should be the end of the story. If I was the person I wanted to be, the story would end there, but it doesn't. James was jacked up about his stupid show, and I had promised to help him. I couldn't say no to my boyfriend."

"I'll file that away."

"Shut up. A week later it was time for me to run the real scam for him, for TV. A friend of ours worked in a bookstore on Hennepin and we asked if they'd let us do a phony book-signing event with fake posters and cameras. James was directing and we had friends doing production. I was presented as a psychic. We had a big poster of my fake book, *Tarot: A Guide to Your Destiny* by Marion Lane—that's my real last name, did you remember that?"

"Of course."

"Wow, you can't lie at all. The poster announced I would be at the bookstore signing books and giving readings for a couple hours on a Friday night. We put the poster up a few days before and put up some fliers. There were no books to sign, so we'd just say that they hadn't come in, but they'd be there next week. I was dressed a little goofier, quite a bit of makeup, sparkles on my eyelids, and a flowing dress that featured the talents. Eccentric, but a real person. I could stay in character easily.

"James was shooting everything. We had a little private area in the bookstore. It was time for the private one-on-one readings—just me, the mark, the cameras, James, and a few friends checking lighting and sound. I started with my tried-and-true opening 'graph. I set up my outs, took some wild guesses, and made a good number of hits. James was worried about the wild guesses. Would some people think I was getting that information from actually being psychic and just deluded into thinking I wasn't psychic? Jesus.

"After each reading James asked them, on camera, how I had done. He asked how suited to them the reading was, and how much it would apply to them alone. They all responded favorably, and I called for the cameras to shut down. The first one we left at that, but I couldn't take it. It was so wrong. In all the others, after James's interview, I demanded he turn off the camera. I took hold of each mark's hand, looked into their eyes, hoping they could see the real me through the blue sparkles, and explained exactly what had just happened. I told them everything.

"I said, 'What you have experienced is called a cold reading. I am not in any way psychic. The techniques I used on you are techniques that all psychics use. It's a psychological profile that all of us respond to. You are not alone. I've said the exact same thing to all these other people, and they responded favorably as well.' In some cases, the crew fed me information they'd overheard, and I confessed to that."

"You have balls."

"I do, they're just higher up. Oh Tiny. Oh Tiny. What you cannot know until you've done it is that when you're reading someone, they trust you. I convinced a man that I was in contact with his dead mother who he had helped care for. The first lady I did cried, and I argued with James about using that. He thought it was good TV, I thought it was a violation."

"How did it end up?"

"Well, it never aired, so it didn't matter that I lost. The more I think about it, I think him insisting on using that crying footage was probably the real reason we broke up, although I blamed it on his affair with the bookstore manager—but I was done with him, when he said her grief was good TV. The manager was kind of cute.

"I read a man who had lost his mom, and when I confessed, I said, 'To me, it is an insult to your memories to have someone tell you that you need them to talk to your mom. I always thought if there were an "other side," then my granny, I loved my granny so much, would do anything possible to contact me and talk to me. She would not need to go through some idiot with blue-sparkle eye shadow who can't come up with any substantial communication and only says, "I'm getting an M." You keep your mom with you in pictures and memories that are so special. I'm telling you this because you seem like a great man. You're fun-loving and good-spirited, and I know this just from our talks before and during the reading. That's what your mom left behind for everyone to see and enjoy. You are part of her, and your relationship is a wonderful legacy. I don't have to be psychic to know all this stuff. I'm just a human being who is being honest with you about what I see.' We said more, but basically that covers what I talked about. We cried some and hugged. I thanked him for being a part of this and for helping me in my fight."

"I've never met anyone like you."

"Is that good or bad? I'm better than my worst day, believe me. Here's the amazing part. My 'confessions' were difficult. I didn't know when I started how people were going to react. The man from the conversation about his mom told me this was the best thing that had happened to him all day. He hugged me and told me what a special person I was to tell the truth. He introduced his lover to me and walked away telling everybody what a great lady I was, and how happy I'd made him. A grandmother brought her family over to meet me, and laughed when I explained how I'd guessed her husband's name. Almost everyone was incredibly happy, and the rest were just fine, if a little bit embarrassed and confused.

"That day I found my answer to people who tell me that skepticism takes the joy out of life, that you need God to experience morality, and that without Him it's just a heartless existence. People were happy to talk. They just wanted someone to listen to their problems or share their hopes and dreams. They wanted to go over funny stories about a loved one they'd lost or just sit and remember them out loud with someone. When I took away the voodoo, what we had shared did not go away. There is all the joy you need in mundane human interaction. I made sure that after we were done, I gave each person a part of me. I had taken away something fake and I needed to replace it with something real. Human contact, human caring, human interaction. I can deliver that. And I try to remember that every day.

"I will never know if I made a difference in them,

but they changed *me*. I went into character as the Tarot Marion Lane, and I never came back to who I was before I was her. I cried all night after my book signing and for the next week I kept crying a lot."

"And you're crying now, and so am I."

"Good you decided to glance up at my face for a change. Sorry, I get flippant when I'm trying to protect myself. I needed you to know who I am over this grilled cheese. This was a few years ago but I'm still recovering. I'll never be the same, and I don't want to be the same. I want to be better.

"I just told you that what you need to do is listen, and then all I did was talk. This has been a monologue. I've needed to tell this story on every date I've gone on. I needed to, but I didn't. No one ever wanted to listen. They wanted to tell me stories about what they had done with their nutty friends in college."

"I didn't go to college."

"How many girlfriends have you had?"

"I don't know, you know . . ."

"It's not a trick question. I don't care. I'm not talking about romance. It's almost rhetorical. You've gone out with women about the same amount as your peers, right? Have you noticed that your friends don't have stories from those women? They maybe have stories about those women, about the dates, maybe about the fucking itself, but have they ever repeated a story to you that they were told on a date?"

"Let me think."

"I bet they haven't. But you do, right? I know you do. You have great stories from women you've dated. Stories you want to tell as your own, tell as if they happened to *you*. Other men don't. Not because they don't go out with interesting women, but because they never find out. I've been around the block and stopped off a few times, I've gone out for a few grilled cheeses, and yet, you're the first man I've told that whole story to. And this is the story about how I was really ready to appreciate you, Tiny. We've both learned, or maybe you always knew, that you can make things better, at least for a little while, just by listening to people. That's important."

You are doing now just what I did with Marion over the grilled cheese. You're paying attention. In a way you are listening. You aren't thinking about what you're going to say next because this is a book. I'm telling you about my life and you're paying attention—that is why I love *you*, my dear reader.

CHAPTER 13

We were both inspired to listen. She wanted to listen next: "How did you get the nickname Tiny?"

I had to eliminate any awkward worries she might have. "Well, fortunately for both of us, I didn't get it in the gym showers."

Fuck, did she laugh! She was laughing hard at my big dick (or at least my not-small dick) and the implication that we were going to fuck. I liked her from first sight, I really dug her story of being a psychic, but now, laughing about my cock, she was the best.

Will Rogers said he never met a man he didn't like. I never met Will Rogers. Howard Stern said that in his early days, he avoided meeting anyone famous, because after knowing them it was too hard to be cruel about them on the radio. I never met Howard Stern. When I listened to Marion, really listened to her, she was fascinating. I liked everything about her. Maybe it was because everyone is fascinating if you get to know them. But Marion was extra-fascinating, and she wanted to fuck Tiny. In a sense, Tiny was a virgin.

Marion was still laughing at my cock, in a good way, when I asked her if we could go to my apartment.

"Slow down, tiger, I got to get back to work. How about I cook you supper at my place tonight?"

"Yeah, and we have to talk about showers and vibrator shopping."

I was feeling great. I was fifteen and a half again. I'd just gotten my driver's license, and I was going to get laid tonight. Even better, I wouldn't have to be in a car parked by the old Troop 5 Boy Scout campground. We'd be in an apartment. I liked being Tiny more than whoever I was before. As a felony murderer I was kinder, and more open to other people. My night with Marion was better than carny sex, and that's not a phrase you hear often. Marion trusted Tiny completely and she had some sex stuff she wanted to try. I guess she found the good parts of a lot of books at her library.

I just wrote several hot paragraphs describing all the hot sex we had in detail, and then I realized that no one is reading this book to cum, so I deleted them. If you're planning on getting off, you can go online and type what you're in the mood for. I can't compete with that. So, suffice it to say, wow.

Marion telling me that long story doesn't mean she was self-absorbed and didn't give a fuck about me. She gave plenty of fucks in every sense. She asked me plenty of questions and she cared about the answers. The difference was I didn't drag on like before I was a murderer. I said a little bit about Greenfield. I told her about learning to juggle. On later dates I played the Residents's *Third Reich 'N Roll* for her. I left out all the felony-murder parts of my life, but I was honest and thorough with her about what I was really thinking and feeling right in the moment. I was there with her. I never wanted to tell those old stories again. Why should I? That life wasn't Tiny's.

CHAPTER 14

I was seriously dating Marion. I had a driver's license. I had a nice little apartment in a friendly little town. I was back to juggling practice every day, and every day I went to the library. Now, when Marion rectified the lower shelves, she was doing it for me. Although she confessed that she'd been doing it for me before, too. One of my favorite parts of sex is that after sex you get to be honest. You get to do the debrief of what you were thinking about each other before you fucked. It's the best. We were almost truly in love. We were almost to where I could ask her to sit on the copy machine to prove it. Maybe I could live like this forever. Maybe I'd run out of money, but I wouldn't get bored with Marion.

I had opened a bank account so I could write checks. They needed a Social Security number. This is a novel, not a tutorial on how to create a fake identity in 1977. I used a very sophisticated trick. I wrote the numbers wicked sloppy and then told jokes while they looked it over. If they ever needed it, they wouldn't be able to read every digit. And every digit mattered. But they would never need it.

I had a bank account. I ordered checks with flowers on them, and thanks to God Almighty and sloppy number writing, I could finally order some decent juggling clubs. I made my first call in Tiny's life to someone who knew me before I was Tiny. I called a juggler in Ohio. I didn't have any address books or notebooks from before, but I remembered his name and the town he was in. I called directory assistance and got his number. I gave him a call. I thought about disguising my voice, but after a few months without yelling and not drinking Chloraseptic, I didn't sound anything like my old dead self anyway.

"Hello."

"Is this Tommy, Tommy Draper?"

"Sure is. Who is this?"

"This is Mick Jackson, I go by Tiny, Tiny Jackson. I'm a juggler and I got your name from an old friend. I know you're a pro juggler. Can I ask you where you get your clubs?"

"Hey, Tiny, nice to know you, no problem, sure. There's a guy in Delaware, works for DuPont, named Stu. If you hold on a second, I have all his info right here, let me dig it up for you. He makes great clubs, a bit pricey, but high quality. You a pro?"

Tommy was a very nice guy for a person, but not an especially nice person for a juggler. All jugglers are super nice. They will invite you over for a barbecue and not ask you to bring anything or clean up. Magicians are all assholes. Mimes get a bum rap, though they're okay people. Puppet people are the worst. But jugglers are all super nice.

"Well, hoping to be pro. Thanks, man, I'd appreciate that. You're the best."

I used to be the closest a juggler got to being an asshole, but not anymore. I was a nice felony-murderer juggler. I got all Stu's information and called him. It was no surprise that Stu was a super nice guy too. I dropped Tommy's name and Stu seemed to really care how Tommy was doing. He said he'd send me a brochure and price list, but I couldn't wait. Now that I was fucking Marion, my top priority was juggling clubs. He described what he was offering, and I told him what I wanted, and paid extra for express shipping. Three hundred and fifty bucks for six clubs. Damn, they were expensive. You had to be a bank robber to be a juggler.

I'm sure he started working on crafting my clubs before he got the check. Why can't the whole world be jugglers? Probably because we need food and shelter, and some assholes need to be magicians.

The clubs arrived, Marion got good at anal, and I still had money left. Except for the malignant cancer in my soul, everything was going just right. The clubs were beautiful, my four was tight, including triples on my double shower. I could flash five every time and I could qualify it a few times in a half hour. I wasn't good enough to make it as a spangle-jumpsuit juggler, but I wasn't ever a serious juggler. I was a comedy juggler.

I had a lot of thinking to do. My hair was long, and I had a beard. I would keep working on growing both even longer over the cold Hibbing winter nights cuddled up with Marion. By spring I would be a different kind of hippie than I'd ever been. I'd look different than I ever looked. The last time I had long hair, I was a teenager and no beard.

It was risky, but I sent off for a mail subscription to the *Philadelphia Inquirer*. Every morning I got up and read that newspaper to see if there was any news about the bank robbers being busted. I couldn't find anything. It was possible Bee and the crew got away clean and no one would even be looking for me. Yet there was no way to be sure.

If Bee hadn't been caught and no one knew he had a talking-white-real-estate-looking guy who was a tall juggler, maybe I could do a few juggling shows. I really wanted to hit the streets. I missed it. But I couldn't do that. No street shows, though there was no harm in doing shows at the Hibbing Y for their stupid boring awards ceremonies, so I did those. I did a few shows at nursing homes and for scout troops. It was nice to get laughs again and I loved having Marion in the audience. I dug it. I was still funny, even with my new voice, and I was a better juggler than ever.

By the turn of the century, people had forgotten Johnny Carson and didn't know Ringo Starr's real name. Would anyone remember a Head House Square juggler with an expensive watch and fancy white clothes even a few months later? Who would be able to recognize the hippie juggler as short-haired juggler a year later? Just as important, would anyone want to? Who cared? But I couldn't take a chance. There was no going back, I was Tiny forever.

If I got famous and someone did some digging, they might find out I was the same juggler as Head House and tie me to the bank robbery. Lucky for me, no juggler has ever gotten famous. You say, "What about W.C. Fields, Johnny Carson, and Steve Martin?" Well, they were famous *despite* being jugglers. I was in no danger there.

The worry was that there weren't many street jugglers back then and they all moved around and knew of each other. I made more money than anyone, and in that small puddle, I was a gigantic pollywog. But I couldn't really be 2good 2B 4got10, could I? How about a Renaissance festival, that isn't exactly street juggling? If I showed up and juggled, would anyone say, "Hey, aren't you that guy who worked the streets in Philly?" Lots of street performers worked the fair(e)s, but would anyone make me? I didn't know. I'm tall, but my voice had changed so much, and I'd be wearing tights. When I was wearing tights, who could look at my face with those legs and that ass available for a gander?

Could I use some of my old routines and lines? Even while I was still working Philly, street performers were already stealing my lines like crazy. And hippies had the sensibility that everything one hippie juggler did belonged to *all* hippie jugglers. I wouldn't mind being seen as a thief if I wasn't seen as the felony murderer who created them. I could start with some of my old lines and just phase those out as I found my new style.

I had about six months to think about it and write a new juggling act before RenFest season, if I decided that was safe. I also had time to lose a little weight so I would look better in tights. The Minnesota Renaissance Festival was one of the biggest in the country. It's a three-and-a-half-hour drive from Hibbing, so I could get home to Hibbing and Marion on weekdays. I'd make way less money with my different, quieter voice and without my tight twelve-minute street act. I'd be a laid-back, seventeenth-century hippie, but maybe I could make a little do-re-mi and get some real laughs and applause.

I went to Marion the next day. "I'm going to wear tights."

"Is this another role-playing thing? Let's give it a try."

I was falling in love.

I told her I was going to try to be a professional juggler at the RenFest. I said it like I'd never done anything like that. She had a dance catalog and helped me order striped red and white tights. A couple weeks later I tried them on for her.

"Um, no," she said. "Didn't you order a dance belt?"

"What's a dance belt?"

"Like a jock strap for dancers. So you don't look like Tom Jones."

"I wish I looked like Tom Jones in tights."

"Nope, not doing a family show. A dance belt will make your crotch look like Ken of Barbie and Ken. That'll be a lot better than Tom Jones for a family show. If you can deliver Tom Jones in tights to me, we can talk. But for now, I'll order you a dance belt. Don't worry, your little ass will still be tight. The wenches will swoon and rip their bodices."

"How do you know so much about concealing cock? Wait, don't tell me. If you're that good at it, keep it up."

I kind of liked the way my cock and balls looked in tights, helped by the optical illusion of the vertical stripes, yet Marion insisted on a dance belt. I had never worn a jock, fuck that shit, I was a hippie; I didn't even wear underwear anymore. The dance belt was very confining. It was like being held tightly in a very strong masculine hand, but not in a good way. It wasn't bad in my living room, though I'd find out soon that after a whole day outdoors in the heat, in tights, the dance belt left my cock and balls as an indistinguishable sweaty Ken mass. I said above that if someone wants to cum, this book isn't for them, they should use the Internet, but if someone is looking for sweaty-dance-belt-in-tights-Renaissance-juggler porn stories, maybe this book is for you. And if someone does masturbate to this book, please let me know. It would make me very happy.

I had tights and a dance belt. I bought some hippie lace-up moccasin boots and then some sort of leather vestlike thing that let my arms show and be very free to juggle. I'd still wear glasses. I suppose contacts would make me look less like the Philly street juggler and more Renaissance, but fuck it. What the fuck was I going to juggle? I got wooden balls (keep your dance belt on and no one will notice). Did I dare do knives? Man, that bank-robber felon juggled knives, and at that time no one else was juggling knives. It seemed too risky.

I called Stu. "Hey, Stu, it's Tiny."

"How are the clubs working out? If there's a problem, let me know and I'll fix it up. I want you happy."

"I'm very happy, Stu. Very happy. I got a question. I'm hoping to work RenFair(e)s. I can't use your beautiful fiberglass clubs there—any ideas?"

"Well, you could do torches. They're no harder to juggle than clubs and I've got some good ones. But is there a lot of flammable hay?"

"Yeah, I know, I've juggled torches, no problem technically. And hay isn't the problem. The problem is that torches look shitty during the day, and you gotta carry around fuel and that's a pain. I don't like carrying stuff. That's why I juggle—to throw things instead of lugging them."

"That's a good one." See? Super nice. "How about knives? There was that loud street guy in Philly who juggled knives, but he's disappeared, so no one is doing knives now."

FUCK FUCK FUCK FUCK FUCK FUCK FUCK.

"Yeah, I heard something about him. I don't want to steal his gag. I was thinking about axes. Could you make me up some nice axe heads, or find them and get me handles that would balance nicely?" FUCK FUCK FUCK FUCK. But I sounded very cool. I didn't tip anything. FUCK.

"Hmmm. There was some Indian"—he meant Native American, but this was the late seventies—"juggler in vaudeville, Chief Something, I think he juggled tomahawks."

"Yeah, let's pretend tomahawks were European Renaissance. Can you make something up? I need them to be able to take a beating, I'll be doing a lot of shows."

"I'll try. Do they need to be sharp at all?"

"Well, sharp enough to stick into a log. I'll need a prover, right?"

"This won't be easy."

"I've got some bread."

"Well, gosh darn it, I like a challenge. What's the price range?"

"You tell me."

CHAPTER 15

Stu did good work. The axes looked great. He used real axe heads, bigger than you might think, and added handles. They looked about as Renaissance as my ass, but they would go with my striped ass to the Renaissance. Right out of the box I could juggle them well, they had a little kick on the spin, the turns not quite even because of the heavy axe heads, but Stu had done a great job. First time picking them up, I did all the juggling moves from my old knife routine without a drop. The juggling was easy. Hovey Burgess, the juggling teacher, used to say to "perform three, practice four." I was pretty good at five, so three was nothing. The axes looked even better than the knives. Juggling in front of a mirror, I liked what I saw. Tiny would have a better act than that loud Philly guy.

Axes looked mean, dangerous, and difficult, but they needed the prover. I had picked up some firewood logs to be ready for practice when the axes arrived. I had a nice big half log that seemed soft. I don't know fucking wood or trees, but it was soft. It was cold in Hibbing, ball-numbing, but I went outside and set my log on the ground (whatever that's slang for, I don't mean that). It wasn't easy, like throwing knives down into a log and having them stick. Knives are nothing, no spin at that distance. But an axe needs a full spin before it hits the log, and that's a lot of wrist. Wrist spin is hard to control and predict. I bounced a bunch of axes off the log. One flew up and hit my knee, MOTHERFUCKER! If I worked on it every day, I'd have some bruises, but I'd learn the spin. They were sharp enough to send me to the ER, but it would have to spin exactly right to stick it into my foot and do permanent damage. Very unlikely. I loved my axes.

I juggled them for Marion that night. "Jesus, be careful, Tiny." Good, she seemed to think there was some honest danger. When I banged them together, she jumped. They had a great scary clang.

When I called Stu to report, he was happy to hear how well they worked. "It was a bastard to find those heads. Those are almost off-the-rack, but I dulled them a bit. They'll stick into a log, but they aren't too sharp. The axe handles that came with them weren't shaped for juggling, but I think the ones I made are good. I think I made a nice grip where they land in your hand. They aren't too heavy, are they?"

"Nope, great."

"I kept them all shiny; you might want to age them a bit. Just knock them around."

"I think I'll do nothing. I've never had to work on making my props look shitty. My knives looked worn after a couple weeks." FUCK FUCK FUCK FUCK.

"I thought you never did knives."

"Not seriously, but I had some juggling knives as a teenager." FUCK.

"Good. Well, I hope you get some use out of these, I had some fun making them. I made a set for myself, but I won't make any for anyone else. You'll be the only jug using these axes."

"That's nice of you, man, but it doesn't matter. The world is big enough for a few axe jugglers. Just don't let them wear tights."

Stu chuckled. "Well, I'm not making any more."

"Thanks, bye."

"Take care, Tiny, don't get blood on your tights."

Oh, dear me, fuck. I guess it ain't no thang, but damn. Maybe this whole getting-back-into-the-juggling-world was a bad idea. Damn. I needed to have a life as Tiny, and Tiny was a juggler.

There were some nice moves that looked good with the axes that didn't mean much with knives. Even just higher throws, like doubles and triples (which I had clean with my four-club half shower), looked great. If I gave the handles a lateral spin, it threw them off-balance and they wobbled, which made them catch the light and glitter. They looked great and looked out of control, but I didn't drop.

Now I had to plan the act. I figured I'd do a crowd gathering to get the folks in, and I'd safely use a lot of my old routine—most of it had been stolen and moved into public domain anyway. No one would know or care that it had started with that loud guy in Philly. Next, my ball routine with wooden balls. I hadn't been woodshedding balls. I wasn't practicing at all, and wooden balls were harder than lacrosse, but by summer I'd be able to get all the same tricks down. My street ball routine was good. I didn't know how much I would have to change up my patter. I started running through the lines, and found that I barely remembered them myself. Who else was going to?

I was one of the first jugglers to comment in a wry way as I juggled. That's what all jugglers do now, but that's not how people juggled before that. The meta thing came in with my g-g-g-generation of j-j-j-jugglers. It wasn't Renaissance style, of course, but since most of the audience didn't know Shakespeare from Tolkien and Roddenberry, I doubted they knew the nuances of juggling history. As for Renaissance nuance, I wouldn't be smelling like shit and raping my prepubescent cousin, so historical accuracy was out ye olde crown-glass window anyway. I was also planning an Andy Warhol joke. So, fuck it.

Most of the knife jokes were fine for axes, though I had to change the vibe. I was a different guy. My Philly street character was so damned loud and aggressive, but Tiny was more of a traditional hippie. I needed an angle to juggle axes as a peacenik. I didn't have to change a lot of the lines, just the delivery. I had to change the thoughts behind the gags.

I had to figure out how to work in the blindfold juggling, and how I could use the blindfold as my collection "hat." It had been part of my great collection pitch. It was good, a big part of the reason I took in so much money. What I came up with was this:

"My final trick is not a juggling trick, but a magic trick. I will take this perfectly ordinary, everyday, black executioner's hood and turn it before your very eyes into a coin purse." Finger snap. "There, it's done. Now, to prove I was totally successful in this transformation, I will need money from each and every one of you. There are a few things to consider when you're deciding how much to give me—note that I say 'how much' and not 'whether or not.'

"First: I am a traveling street performer, I have to travel light, and I have found that bills are much lighter than coins.

"Second: I am six foot seven inches tall, and I have three sharp axes and an excellent memory for faces—you can pay me some money now, or all your money later on the way to your car.

"Third: if you didn't see the whole show, that's no excuse, this is the best part—but people in the very back row, you needn't pay a penny, but I request one thing from you: join your hands in a symbolic gesture of brotherhood . . . and don't let anyone in front of you pass without giving me money."

Then I'd drop down to wicked humble and say, "Thank you very much," almost quietly. I would hold the bow for a while. Make them see me as a serious performer and not a beggar. I didn't want to rush for the coin. I wanted to make people know that they were waiting to give me money, not because I made them feel like they should but because I deserved it and they wanted to give me the money.

It's a money finish. It was less Renaissance than my glasses and my Lycra/nylon-blend tights, but I didn't care about that. I didn't care about anachronisms. I had one worry: Would anyone remember that hunk, word for word, from Philly? And if they did, would they think I'd just stolen it like most variety artists would? That was a matter of life or life in prison.

Another thing worried me: In order to do that finish, I needed my "executioner's hood." That meant presenting the image of a tall performer, standing with a bag over his head, juggling sharp implements. A memorable image, maybe *too* memorable? And with a bag over my head, my beard and hair wouldn't be visible to pull their focus. Maybe I shouldn't use a dance belt, so they'd have something to distract them. Maybe I should call Tom Jones for a transplant.

My last two tricks, the most important in my show (other than crowd gathering and money collection), was the hood stuff. I would bring a woman up from the audience, and juggle in front of her while she wore the blindfold. It had to be a woman to be small enough to do safely, and it was too creepy with a child. That was a nice trick, but it also served to prove that the blindfold was real, which it wasn't. (Notice how quickly I told you that? I told you way back the first time I mentioned it—I would have made such a shitty magician. I would have had to just talk while another guy did all the work.)

Juggling inside the hood was a very tranquil experience. The hood was a thick black velvet bag sewn inside a thinner shiny black bag. They were only sewed together on one side. When I put the bag over a punter's head to juggle around her, she was seeing into deep black velvet; she couldn't see a thing. It was clear that it was opaque to her, and therefore to the audience. When I put it over my own head to juggle, I turned it around and put my head in with only the thin, almost transparent cloth in front of my eyes. With all the light on the outside, people couldn't see my face through it, yet I could see out into all the light through just a thin veil. Juggling is so tactile and peripheral. I didn't have to think about script. There were no lines now. I didn't have to think about juggling. This was my time to look at people. The exhibitionist becomes the voyeur. The people stood there gobsmacked, etching the image into their memories, and getting ready to applaud and give me money. It was a transcendent time. A time when I really felt beautifully alone in a crowd with a bag on my head yet still the center of attention. I could stare at attractive women, and I could watch the children in front and the men while their guards were down.

It was a very strong finish, then right into the money pitch with a snap of my fingers. Most of the show was original, though I also did the apple eating—eating an apple while juggling it along with two knives. It's a standard trick (that just means it was stolen so long ago and so often that the original guy doesn't have a chance, like Beethoven, Lenny Bruce, and the Velvet Underground [that's a bill I want to see]). Apple eating while juggling is easy but amazing, very sloppy, and you get to talk with your mouth full and spit all over the front row. I would mock them, saying, "*Oh yeah, let's run over and get good seats.*" That take was my own idea, but the idea of eating an apple while juggling was someone else's, probably Velvet Lenny Beethoven's.

I had all winter to think about the act. I told Jack LaLanne at the Y that I was going be practicing with axes (I didn't want him to be surprised), but I had gym mats all over to protect the floor. The wooden balls took less time to get tight and clean than I'd expected. As a felony murderer I was a better juggler than I was as a regular juggler, no doubt about that.

Because of my style of commenting on the juggling while being totally outside it, I couldn't drop. The juggling had to be perfect. Most jugglers drop once or twice a show and it's no harm. They're showing off, and small mistakes just make it look harder. But I was doing something more complicated. All my lines were from the POV of watching the juggling, not doing it. The opposite of showing off. The juggling had to be just automatic. If I dropped and had to bend over to pick up, the illusion that I was outside the act, above the act, was destroyed. I couldn't allow people to think the juggling was any problem at all. I didn't even want them to picture me practicing. One of my lines seemed to contradict that: "I bothered to learn this, you're going to watch it." But there's no contradiction. For that line to be funny, you must understand it intellectually, while not believing viscerally that I practiced at all. Consequently, nothing could be a strain, or a reach. Not only could I not drop, but I could also not really save a bad throw. No effort. The person speaking was much too sophisticated to practice juggling. The whole juggling act was an apology for the juggling act.

After a few weeks in the gym, I was finding the places where those jokes could live. Tiny was not too sophisticated to juggle, like the Philly guy—Tiny was just too detached and distracted to juggle. Not a stoner, but someone who tried to live if not on the astral plane, then at least a higher plane. All the same lines started to feel okay. It felt like Tiny could land these jokes.

My voice was a whole other thing. I felt I could play to a hundred punters outdoors in the wind without screaming. That's fewer than a quarter the number I played to in Philly. Loud, but not pushing. In the fog of my future little juggling war, I might want to push and go louder, but I had to avoid that. If I screamed, I was instantly the guy in Philly, a felony juggler who had to go back to the doctor and then to prison. I had to hold back.

I was ready for Tiny's Renaissance.

CHAPTER 16

My super-expensive James Bond digital watch alarm went off in the Shakopee motel at eight in the morning. All the other Renaissance hippies camped on the grounds. I was done sleeping rough. I'd done my time without a proper toilet and shower. My motel was near the grounds. Marion hadn't come with me; I didn't want her there. She could come next week or the week after. I needed time to find out who Renaissance Tiny was. My Datsun 210 station wagon that got me all around Hibbing also got me all the way down south to Shakopee.

On the drive I ran my RenFest act a few times in what was my new definition of "full voice." The cassette player was rotating *The Third Reich 'N Roll*, *Fingerprince*, and *Not Available*, all by the Residents, some goofy Dylan bootlegs, and *Never Mind the Bollocks, Here's the Sex Pistols* when I wasn't doing my act for the windshield.

I got in the afternoon of the day before the

fair(e), went to the office, and got my parking pass, rules for performers to ignore, and the schedule. I knew where the office was. A month earlier I'd driven down, auditioned on the site, and driven back to home sweet Hibbing in the same day. It wasn't a bad drive. I hadn't been worried much about the audition, but now that the first day was here, I was a bit nervous. I hadn't been in front of a crowd for a while. When you're learning to play jazz, your first goal is to not be noticed and your second goal is to be noticed. My life had been like that: I spent almost a year making sure I wasn't noticed. Now I was being directed where to park by a high school student in a heavy metal T-shirt under a burlap tunic, in a dusty field, and I was nervous. In a little over an hour, I was going to work on being noticed. Just a little. Just in a field in Minnesota. Just a little noticed.

With my schedule came a map of the grounds. My first show was at what in my carnival days was called "a doniker location." "Doniker" was carny slang for what was euphemistically labeled a "toilet." The doniker location was right near those disgusting portable outhouses. No one would ever trust me with state secrets, but if a fool did and the bad guys wanted to crack me, fifteen minutes in a Circus Vargas doniker and I'd promise to fly a plane into the World Trade Center myself just to get out of that doniker. A friend once invited me to go to Circus Vargas on a whim. I was wearing sandals and I had to stop and buy shoes and socks to put on just in case I had to piss.

My first show at the doniker location was ten

thirty at the opposite end of the grounds from the gate, which opened at ten. Who walks into a fair(e) and heads right to the far side without even stopping for a Scotch egg and ye olde coffee? That's okay. I had to find my street legs again anyway.

I started my crowd gathering. Then I repeated that with the people who had just run up. To people entering the fair(e), it sounded like a very exciting show was going on at the far side of the grounds. I would say it worked like a charm, but charms don't work. It worked just like my street days, and I got a bigger crowd than I expected. In just a few minutes I had about fifty people sitting on hay bales (humanity only started baling hay in the late 1800s, so my Lycra tights and Warhol jokes were fine).

The opening—standing there encouraging people to cheer at nothing, then laughing at the people who ran to see what they were missing—was over. It was time to juggle. Being in tights was weird. I was glad I had my dance belt on. I was self-conscious enough with the shape of my ass being so crystal clear. I had an apple and my half log full of Stu's handcrafted still-too-shiny juggling axes by my side. I reached into my executioner's hood and pulled out my three wooden balls. It wasn't a good idea to use the same crowd gathering, or to use the hood, but this was the first show of my first weekend—the first time Tiny had ever done a show not at the YMCA, and he needed all the help he could get. The chance that one of these fifty people had seen the street act in Philly was approaching zero. I felt I was safe, so I pretty much did the act from Head House except with wooden balls, axes, and a clearer and quieter voice. The fifty self-chosen bale-sitters had no problem hearing me.

Holy fuck it felt good. I was getting big laughs and loud applause. I was killing. I would phase out the Philly material as I grew more confident and even replace the hood, but it was a great act. I passed my hood and made $48.77. Even though I said my old line, "If you want your children hurt badly, send them up with pennies, I don't think it's cute," I got some pennies. I did think it was cute.

I had auditioned to just work for tips. Top salary was a hundred bucks a day and they wouldn't give that to a fucking new guy from the seventeenth century anyway. That kind of coin wasn't worth having to fudge my Social Security number. Cash was my friend. Who cares? I didn't need the extra buck. I was scheduled for eight shows a day. This doniker show was most likely my slowest show of the day, so I could very conservatively estimate fifty bucks a show. Take out motel, gas, a few Scotch eggs, a few greasy turkey legs, and a funnel cake a day, and I'd get back to Marion with thirteen hundred bucks or so. Since I was counting chickens that had barely been laid, over the whole festival I'd clear about seventy-five grand, a very good yearly income for Hibbing in 1977. I could live like this for a while.

Marion suggested I bang a few wenches, and I didn't push to find out if she meant it; I would assume she meant it and that she might even help get some ass for me. I had to adjust my libido. I was very used to tight jeans and a T-shirt with no bra getting me excited. In Shakopee I would have to focus on cleavage for miles and breasts sitting on a corset plate like a deli platter and long flowing skirts. I could learn to dig on that. Especially if the corsets were leather.

CHAPTER 17

I love you, honey, but the season's over. I suggested we have a private rock show at the end of the festival to cleanse ourselves of crumhorns, lutes, and bagpipes. I asked the owners if we could use their generators, so we could make some serious twentieth-century noise. The owners loved me because I hadn't cost them a farthing, and the punters had all been talking about me. They were telling their friends to go see the juggler at the fair(e). I was featured heavily in a couple newspaper stories and I even did a TV spot. I asked them not to quote from my act and to please choose a picture that wasn't with the executioner's hood. I just did the apple eating on TV, and everyone does that. No one could recognize me from any of this.

We had power all night for our closing party. The generators at RenFests are always powerful and reliable because all RenFests really do is sell soda and beer. Everyone's just working to get people to buy drinks. A wise man once told me to find out what business people were really in. The Rolling Stones are T-shirt salesmen, that's where they make most of their money. RenFest owners are selling beverages. They can let vendors own and operate their own hippie belt stands and macramé, they don't need a taste. The gate pays for all advertising, rent, and staff. Small-time entrepreneurs can negotiate to own a turkey leg concession or set up funnel cakes, but the investors always keep the drinks—that's where all the money is. I was a worker who brought people in to buy Coke and I cost them nothing. We could have the generators for a night. Keep us working peasants happy.

I had met a few coworkers who played electric guitar, in the seventies everyone did. One of the potters from town played drums. He had a drum kit with double kicks. I needed it to be a proper rock drum kit; I had had enough of djembes. The drummer had to be a local to have a kit he could get to the grounds. A few of the grounds crew cobbled together a temporary stage. Someone had a PA, and we didn't need lights.

There was lots of drinking and drugs for the others, and we set up the rock band by bonfire light. The band members were all younger than me. We had about fifteen backup singers from all the king's choral groups. There was a sixteen-year-old madrigal boy who played bass well. I borrowed his bass in the middle of the party and sang "Ye Olde Wilde Thing" and "Walk on Ye Olde Wilde Side," just Weird

Al–type song parodies where I ad-libbed lyrics. It wasn't the Renaissance anymore, so we rocked out with our cocks out. There were no rehearsals, we just played what everyone knew. It was a huge success because there were no bagpipes. I believe the closing-rock-show-around-a-bonfire tradition lasted for many years after me; they might still do it today. I heard they now sing "Wild King" instead of my lyrics, thinking it's cleverer. Fuck that, too on the nose.

On Saturday of the last weekend, the owners invited me to come back and perform the following year and offered me some money on top of my "hats." Good, I had some bargaining power. I said I didn't need them to pay me, but I wanted reserved parking and a place to lock up my money and props between shows. I also wanted my choice of stages and times, and I wouldn't do the fucking parade. It was an easy negotiation. They didn't need my Social Security number for reserved parking.

Marion had come down with me two of the weekends to see my shows and have fun. Away from the library and 207 miles from where anyone might know her, oh my goodness. She was no longer a librarian. Again, if you want porn go to the web, it's what it was created for, but I fingered her, and she blew me on the drive. She had gotten herself quite a wench outfit. I didn't describe Marion earlier, but she was short, just over five feet, so we had some serious sexual dimorphism going on. She was traditionally pretty minus zero no limit. She had that Sally Fields *Smokey and the Bandit*/Linda Ronstadt look. Her eyes were a better blue than mine. She had pale-blue eyes that would have made Lou Reed even more melancholy as they cut through his ennui. She was not leggy, but she had a huge rack, and most importantly she loved her big breasts. All that really matters sexually about breasts is how much the owner enjoys them, and she enjoyed every milligram. I have big hands, but they couldn't hold even the amount of breast that showed above the top of her corset, and no one liked that more than she.

The first weekend she saw all eight of my shows both days. I was thinking up new lines and bits to differentiate myself from the Philly guy, yet with Marion in the audience I didn't want to work on those new lines. I wanted to kill. I pretty much did the exact Philly act in tights with axes. I wanted her to see me destroy a big crowd, so I pushed the voice a bit. I did a little screaming but kept it under control.

While I was counting my money, she was happily reaching into the sweaty mass that was inside my dance belt. It didn't matter what she did, no matter how hard she got me, that dance belt would scrunch it up and conceal it. I would not be challenging Tom Jones.

When she wasn't out fetching Scotch eggs and turkey legs for us to gorge on between shows, she was chatting up wenches: "Hey, you've been camping out here for weeks, right? Do you know the juggler in the striped red tights? The big loud one? He and I have a motel room with a nice hot shower. After the fair(e) closes tonight, want to (she was a librarian, she didn't say 'wanna') come with us? We'll go out to supper. Come back to the room. We'll all have a nice hot shower to get the festival off us, and then . . . well, we can see what happens. Would you like that?" She was way out of Hibbing, she didn't fucking care. She was very successful with the women. That was fun.

After a couple of wenches, she asked if it would be okay to ask a guy or two back to the room with us.

I said, "Sure, I'm down for that. We've had a lot of fun talking about that. I wasn't bullshitting. Give it a try."

"*Try?* Did you just say *try?* Did you really say *try?* You said *try.* Would you take a look at what I'm featuring here? Have you gone blind? *TRY? TRY?*"

"Oops. Um. Yeah. Oops."

"Yeah, if I ask, it's going to happen. That's why I want to make sure you're not bluffing. There are a couple guys I was considering sneaking out behind the tents with, but there's that lack-of-shower thing. Everyone here really needs a shower. With the wenches, I lead with the showers. With the guys, I don't think I have to even mention the shower. Their showers will be for me."

I wasn't bluffing. We had a blast. The weekends she was there, bringing wenches and jesters to my shows, I kept the shows good. I did all the Philly stuff and blasted it out. She wasn't there the last two weekends, but I didn't really have time to change up the act. She couldn't make the final rock party, she had an early morning at the library, so I was there blowing out my voice alone, screaming rock and roll for her so loud I'm sure she could hear me in Hibbing.

I drove back home late the next morning with my pipes really blown out. I couldn't talk right, but I had no one to talk to. I stopped at a drugstore and got some Chloraseptic. I didn't drink it, of course, but I sprayed it in as I drove and screamed along with Johnny Rotten. I felt like a pro again.

CHAPTER 18

That went on for another three years. My show changed a little over time, but I never developed the whole new show I had planned. I would rest my voice in the offseason, but it stayed a bit funky year-round. My offseason got shorter as I drove way down to the Texas Renaissance Festival. The Texas fair(e) went a few weeks longer than Minnesota, so I picked up those weeks after Minnesota closed. I even got out to Maryland one year, and tried the Florida fair(e) as well. We timed Florida with Marion's vacation time so she could join me. Maid Marion's motel showers had become legendary and nationwide. She no longer had to invite, she just had to field inquiries, and explain, "Sorry, no alcohol or drugs."

Marion and I moved in together. During the eight and a half months or so that I had off every year, I would juggle at the Y and go to the library, where I would read and watch Marion work, waiting for her to rectify the lower shelves. My juggling was really improving, though I didn't change any juggling in the RenFest act. I just couldn't find a way to make money with ye olde five-club back-crosses. When I had to think too much about doing the trick, I wasn't funny. I wasn't mostly a juggler, and I never wanted to be primarily a juggler. I did do the harder juggling at all the local events, and people didn't get sick of me. Working as an amateur, I could do tough tricks, drop occasionally, and be pleasantly funny. These were fun unpaid shows, so I didn't have to be perfect.

Marion and I had friends who we hung out with. We didn't get kinky with anyone except each other in Hibbing. We didn't want to be the creepy couple of the world's largest open-pit iron mine. We got our freak on in the privacy of our bedroom and, of course, at RenFests around the country. A couple times she fucked my brains out in the stacks during library hours, and she loved to flash in public, but we never got caught. I didn't get a thrill out of that, it just made me nervous, but she loved it, so what the hell? We were normal Minnesotans, no more adventurous than Bob Dylan, Prince, or Judy Garland.

This seemed like our lives, and we loved it. The Internal Revenue Service was led to believe we lived entirely on Marion's library salary. The RenFests never paid me a salary, but I kept all my tips. That was all cash, and that was the money we spent. We didn't get caught with extra income, and we didn't get caught flashing her nipples at McDonald's. Life was good.

* * *

One afternoon show during the last weekend of the Minnesota RenFest, I looked through the hood as I juggled my axes, letting my mind and my gaze wander over the crowd. Alone and the center of attention, my height exaggerated by the big blindfold over my head and the vertical red stripes of my tights, I twisted the worn axes to catch the sunlight and disco-ball through the audience. This exciting and terrifying image, the climax of my show, had made me enough money in ten weekends to only have to pretend to live off a librarian's salary. Marion herself wasn't there that weekend, so I'd gotten enough sleep. She was visiting her parents up north. But I'd see her on Tuesday.

I'd left my car in its designated parking place, and the Scotch eggs guy slipped me mine without my having to wait in line. I'd made bank my first three shows and the money was safely locked up, and I had apples for the rest of the shows that day. The whole weekend had been great. I'd checked out of the motel, and after my last show I'd drive directly home, listening to some Clash, and be in Hibbing before midnight.

I scanned the audience as the axes flew in front of my hooded face. I wasn't checking out the women; I was watching a young father lovingly soothe his baby in a stroller, kind of ignoring me. I loved that. I loved seeing what was important in life. I let my gaze drift a bit deeper into the crowd . . .

And the axes just fell. All three. It was my first drop ever doing that trick, and it was as bad as it gets. All the axes hit the deck. One of them might have cut my leg. I didn't know. I didn't feel anything. I heard a few gasps in the crowd, yet there was only one thing I saw. I saw Bee. He wasn't wearing wings. He had no cape. He didn't look like James Brown. I don't really know what he was wearing. Before I had even consciously recognized him, the axes had dropped. The hood started to suffocate me; I couldn't breathe through the translucent cloth. I stood there frozen for a few moments, and then finally ripped off the hood. My eyes met Bee's for an instant before he turned to the guy next to him and nodded. And walked away. Vanished into the Renaissance.

The show must go on. The only reason they say that is because it feels like it does. My show should have ended, though it didn't. I don't know what I said. I probably said, "Sometimes jugglers will miss on purpose to make it seem hard . . . That wasn't one of those times." That's just a guess. I have no way of knowing. I remember nothing.

Some words came out of me, words always come out of me. I'm a white guy who can talk. I did my money pitch. I passed the hood. I got my money. I did it all without being there. I was just staring at where Bee had been. I should have looked at the guy next to him who he had nodded to. I should have done a lot of things, but mostly I should not have done any shows after Philly, ever.

CHAPTER 19

Could I disappear again? I was Tiny more than I'd ever been the other guy. I loved being Tiny. I had told Marion nothing about my past. She thought my parents and sister were dead and that was true, but the old me she didn't know about was also dead. I had no ties to anyone but her. She was my life. I knew I should have walked away from that RenFest show like I walked away from the bank robbery. I could have slipped behind a burlap-covered dumpster, shaved my beard, and cut my hair (it was now almost down my back). I could have thrown away the hippie clothes and been, *what*? What was left? There's the real estate guy and the hippie, what else could I be? The Village People were just starting up, maybe I could be the Native American, or the cowboy. I'd need a Social Security number to join the military or be a policeman, and I'd need skills to be the construction guy. Wait, I guess I could have also been the leather daddy. But I didn't become any of those—although in retrospect, leather daddy might have been nice.

Like an idiot, an idiot in love, I drove back to Hibbing to see Marion. Some of the ride I was just absent, like I was on a train. Some of the ride, I rehearsed a hundred speeches I could give to Marion. I could explain everything, and we could run together. Who would we be running from? It couldn't be the police; Bee was in street clothes. They wouldn't have brought him halfway across the country just to finger me. Who was next to him? Some guy. I should have paid attention, but I was in shock. I couldn't even juggle three axes in a simple cascade, for Christ's sake; I sure couldn't commit a stranger's face to memory.

Why was Bee there and who was he with? It was a white guy, right? A white guy who needed to take talking lessons from me? I hadn't seen anything anywhere about Bee's crew, my crew, getting busted. I was a long way from Philly, but I got the Philly paper and I was in the library and in the librarian every day. I checked the periodicals like crazy. Busting bank-robbing felony murderer would be news. Never mind, Bee was in street clothes. He couldn't want money from me. I hadn't taken any money. Maybe Bee had just wanted to see my street show again and then split because he didn't like it and didn't want to give me money. Nope. What the fuck?

I pulled up to our little house in Hibbing. It was the middle of the night, and the door was open. Not just unlocked, but open. September is fucking cold in Minnesota, what was Marion thinking? Wait, Marion *wasn't* thinking. Marion wasn't there. Marion was up north (fact: there are places north of Hibbing) to visit her mom and dad for the weekend. She had Monday off from the library. We weren't planning to see each other until tomorrow night when she got back home. I knew that. Why was the door open? Maybe now was the time to shave, cut my hair, and pull a Houdini. I could be a leather daddy heading for the West Village before Marion got home. Fuck. Marion. Whoever was standing next to Bee in my crowd and was now in my house would have gotten our address from the RenFest office. Whoever was standing next to Bee didn't need my Social Security number. Unlikely he was a good guy. So, a bad guy had the address where Marion lived with me. Well, I guess I wouldn't be paying hot twinks in the Village to suck my cock after all.

In the movie version everything would go black right now, and the next scene I'm tied to a chair in my own house. What did happen was just as scary, but less dignified. I wasn't hit over the head. The guy who had been standing next to Bee was now walking out of my house, walking toward me. I turned to run toward the car, and he simply shook his head no. I stood there frozen, like a white guy who couldn't talk.

"Poe?"

"Not really, no. Not anymore."

"It wasn't a question."

"Well, your voice went up a bit at the end, so I was confused." I could talk again.

"You are a hard man to find, but we were made

to do hard things. Come inside, we need to talk. My name is Jerry."

We walked inside together. He didn't drag me, he didn't hit me, we just walked inside. He told me to take a seat in my own house. He had been nondescript at the fair(e), but the more I looked, the more scared I got. His head was shaved, which was less common back then—I guess he wasn't nondescript at all, I just didn't look that closely while I was in shock. He had a beard, long, but trimmed nicely and full, unlike mine. He wasn't tall, he was short, though he was built like a fucking cement pylon. He was wearing a tie and suit jacket; the sleeves were pushed up and I could see jail-house ink. This is way back in the time before every eighteen-year-old girl had tattoos from her wrist to her perky pink breasts. His tattoos weren't like that. Oh dear. Dennis the Menace on a motorcycle flipping the finger to the world was tattooed where a watch would be. And in India ink *F.T.W* and *1%* on the other wrist. I knew those meant *Fuck the World* and *99% outlaw/1% citizen*. The tattoos were so sloppy. Awful artwork, but it communicated everything I needed to know. That's successful art. I was fucked.

"Here's the deal. I don't want to fuck you up. I don't. Beating up someone like you doesn't get my cock hard. It's just my job, and I'm a lazy bastard. I'd rather just walk away with what I need and take the rest of the night off. Take the rest of the night to beat up someone who *will* get my cock hard. So, give me what I came for and we're done. You'll never see me again. You can go back to playing hippie juggle-boy."

"I don't know what you came for."

SMACK! He hit me with his fist, right in my face. I wasn't ready for that. I didn't even move my face out of the way. I hardly saw his hand move. And he hit me hard. I felt that iron taste of blood in my mouth. I thought about spitting it out, but I thought he might see that as disrespectful and hit me again. I sucked it off my lip and swallowed it. I liked the taste, it was sexy, though I didn't like the pain.

"I saw some pictures; your wife looks like she'd be someone I'd enjoy beating up. Maybe this *will* be a fun day at work."

There was no reason to explain to him that we weren't married and had an open relationship. I'd just get smacked again. Instead, my plan was to piss myself in fear and cry a little. That was the only thing on my agenda. He didn't have a weapon. I wasn't tied up. I could just stand up and kung-fu him. I could just do that like I could just climb Everest with neither sherpa nor oxygen while learning calculus. I didn't even really dare to bring my hands to my face to see how much damage he'd already done.

"Please tell me what you came for and I'll try to give it to you."

"Are you that stupid?"

"Yes, I'm that stupid. I'm stupider than that stupid. Way stupider. Please spell it out for me."

"You have a book with my boss's personal information in it. Just a little notebook. It's worth less than a dollar at Woolworths, but it's worth your life and the life of your cunt wife right now."

"Listen, really, honestly, I don't know anything about your boss's notebook. I don't know."

"You're not honest. That's my point. But you're going to be honest eventually; why not be honest now? I'm going to beat the shit out of you. And then I'll beat the shit out of your wife, and more, and then come back to you. And I'll keep doing that. I won't get tired. There's only one way to stop that from happening."

"This is connected to the bank robbery with Bee, right?"

"Yeah, Bee got real honest real fast, not a stupid man. He said you had the notebook, and then we spent more time finding you than I spent finding him. Now we found you, and now you give me the notebook."

"Bee told you I had the notebook?"

"You either have the notebook or you traded it to the feds or someone worse in exchange for some witness protection. But that seems unlikely. What witness protection would put you in the same goofy job just in a different state? A beard isn't a disguise. Your show sucks, by the way. The blindfold is fake."

"You wouldn't have known that if I hadn't happened to see Bee through it. That's what tipped it. How did Bee say I got the notebook?"

"Your bullshit bank robbery boosted the content of seven safe deposit boxes."

"Is it 'safe deposit' or 'safety deposit'? No one seems to know."

"I might enjoy beating the fuck out of you."

"Sorry. I joke when I'm nervous." Would joking get me hurt more or less?

"Bee split up the shit from the safeTY deposit boxes, and the notebook was in your share. There is no value in that notebook other than to give it to me and not get beat to shit."

I was figuring this out. There were only seven safe(ty) deposit boxes they emptied? Bee was stupid and misguided but fair. I guess there had been seven people involved in the heist, so he gave each of his criminals the contents of one box. Lucky me, I had gotten the mobster jackpot. Fuck. I had never even shown up for that meeting. I was already on a train to Hibbing when the meeting was supposed to happen. I was already Tiny. I figure Bee gave my share to another guy to give me at the meeting. He either didn't show up in order to rip me off, or when I didn't show up, he thought, *Bank error in my favor, collect the fucking notebook of death*. No one knew I hadn't been at that meeting except the guy and me. No one else knew. When the heat came on, he must have just said he'd given me my share, including the cursed notebook, and he was done. He was probably happy now. He probably wasn't sitting in his own piss in a chair in his own house.

"I never showed up for the meeting, I never collected my share. Never. I never met the guy to give me my share."

"Oh, I see. You robbed a bank, but not for the money. You rob banks as a public service? You rob banks pro bono?"

"I had plenty of money and I was scared."

"So, if you had plenty of money and you were scared to rob a bank, why didn't you *not* rob a bank? That's what most people do."

"It was kind of peer pressure, I guess. We were at a Burger King and—"

SMACK! He punched me in the face again. Holy fuck! This was real. Fuck.

"I'll tell you one thing: your hot little chicky in Philly sure didn't know where you put your share. I don't think she even knew you robbed a bank."

"Fuck, she didn't. She didn't know anything. Nothing. Is she okay?"

"She'll be fine. She'll need a little counseling, and I wouldn't call her ever again if I were you."

I can talk, so I tried a new tack: "I didn't know the value of the notebook. I had no idea. He just gave me money and a bag of stuff. I sold the stuff that had value, like pearls and stuff, and the notebook didn't mean anything." I watched his face like I watched my crowds. I was trying to get a sense of how this was playing. Reading his next sentence would be life and death. I better play it right.

"I don't give a fuck about pearls—you could have stuck them up your ass for all I care."

"I've never tried that, like the knotted-handkerchief thing? Is it fun?"

SMACK! The pain overwhelmed the sexy taste. Well, he didn't like that answer, but I wasn't sunk yet.

"I need the notebook."

Okay, so whatever was written in this notebook

was needed. They needed it for something. I couldn't just try to convince them that it was destroyed. I had to convince him that I had the notebook, and it was somewhere far enough away that I'd have time to think and protect Marion and me, maybe in that order. Maybe I really cared about her.

I knew that he'd come all the way to Minnesota with Bee to find me. He was willing to travel. If I could get him to travel, maybe I could look for an opportunity. I had to get him the fuck away from Marion. He seemed competent. That's good. Someone trusted him completely. I bet he didn't show his work, I bet he just got the job done. I was going to be betting my life on that. Betting my life on Jerry not having documented all his work.

I love the Three Stooges. I had been talking to a Stooge head about how many of their sketches were ripped off other vaudeville and burlesque guys. There was a thing Moe, the leader, did with Mike Douglas when that goofy Philly afternoon-talk-show guy had people like John and Yoko as cohosts for a week. He had Moe Howard on the show (not the same show, not a Stooge and a Beatle together, sadly), and my friend was talking about the "Niagara Falls" sketch. "Slowly I turned, step by step, inch by inch." That was a standard vaudeville bit that lots of acts did. A guy heard "Niagara Falls" and started going mental. He would say, "Niagara Falls, slowly I turned, step by step, inch by inch," and then grab the guy who said it and start beating up the knucklehead. Anyway, I had been thinking about Niagara Falls.

Niagara Falls was far away from Hibbing. I'd been there once with my parents when I was twelve. All I remember is the *Maid of the Mist*, the boat we went on right into the falls and the gift shop. I was going to have to do a lot of talking. And it had to be my best talking ever.

"Niagara Falls."

"What?" He didn't turn slowly, and step by step, inch by inch, move toward me. I guess that was good, although if he had done the bit, it might have been funnier.

"You don't need to beat me or fuck up my wife." I liked calling her my wife. "I believe you need the notebook, and I don't even want it. Your notebook is in Niagara Falls. Right after the meeting where I got the stuff, I took the cash and headed up to Niagara Falls. I wanted to cross the border into Canada, in case the other guys got caught—I'd be safer there from the police."

"Why Niagara Falls?"

"One-fifth of the fresh water in the world goes over that dam."

"What?"

"Right, I've never understood that. It can't be one-fifth at the same time, and if they mean over time, wouldn't all the fresh water in the world eventually go over the falls? I mean with rain and evaporation and shit? In geological time it has to be 100 percent, right?"

"Where is it in Niagara Falls?"

"I'll give you the exact address. It's in a locker

with the other stuff. I have it written down, and you can go get it. And we're done, right?"

He smacked me. Fuck, I hated that. I really don't like being hit.

"I'm not your errand boy."

"Then I'll go get it and . . . mail it to you?"

SMACK! Fuck.

"We are going to Niagara Falls together to get the notebook. If you give me the notebook, and I'm convinced that there are no copies, you go free. If you are lying to me and take me to Niagara Falls to lie to me more, I will let you know what a bad idea that was. And your cunt wife too. This will have been the worst idea of your life. You better give me that notebook in Niagara Falls."

Slowly I turned—step by step—inch by inch.

I had just under a thousand miles to kill Jerry.

CHAPTER 20

I didn't hear Jerry ever make a phone call to Bad Guy Central. There were no cell phones or texting yet. Jerry did seem to have some other magic fucking evil notebook he was keeping notes in, but who else saw that? I'm sure he knew where to find Bee. I'm sure he knew where to find all the other guys in our crew, but maybe Jerry hadn't told anyone else in his organization. I was guessing, hoping. Truth is, I was praying that if Jerry died, everything would die with him. The bad boss would replace Jerry, yet it might take awhile for the new bad guy to get up to speed. Maybe long enough for Marion and me to be other people.

You know I had never killed anyone. I was a felony murderer, I *am* a felony murderer, but I had never even hit anyone in anger. I add "in anger" because sex play and comedy, but I'd never been in a fight. Never. I'd been beat up a few times, in anger and with very little sex and comedy, but I was such a peacenik that I just let the guy beat me until he got tired. I'd always thought that I wouldn't even kill to protect myself. I pulled that knife to stop that rape, but I was bluffing. I trashed his house, though that doesn't count. I didn't hurt him. I'm just a talker.

I never want evildoers to be punished. I want them to be stopped from doing evil. They can stay evil for all I care, they just have to be stopped from expressing it. We need prisons, but they should be as safe and comfortable as practical. I'm fine if they're country clubs, they can bowl every night if they like, if the rest of us are protected. I keep using the word "evil," but I don't believe in evil. There is no such thing as an evil force. Evil is a cop-out that takes responsibility off the perpetrators. What we think of as evil is just people who are wrong. Misguided people making very bad decisions. Fuck "evil." I don't even believe in free will. That's just a lie we live with like the lie that there are colors out in the world.

I don't believe in the death penalty. I don't believe in war. Yet now that the bullet was hitting my boner, I had found a situation where I was willing to kill someone. I'm sure there was a lot good about Jerry. I'm sure Jerry was mostly good. None of us should be defined by the worst things we've done. That's a self-serving moral position for a felony murderer, but I think I believe it. Jerry deserved to live. He deserved to be happy. I had no reasonable argument for killing Jerry, but I was going to.

Jerry thought I was afraid of him. I *was* afraid of

him. He thought I was a fucking pussy. I *am* a fucking pussy. But I didn't like the idea of Marion being raped and beaten. I didn't like the idea of either of them together or separately. I didn't even like the idea of me being beaten with or without being raped. I didn't like whatever he had done to Tracy, my Philly girlfriend, though I wasn't willing to punish him for any of that. I was willing, however, to stop him from doing it again. I couldn't think of any way to stop him other than killing him. My poverty of imagination would lead to Jerry's death.

I couldn't call the police. How would that work? I call the police and tell them I'm being held against my will. They come and find us, and I say he's trying to get a notebook from me that I don't have from a bank that I robbed? I'd be willing to do the time in prison even though I don't like bowling, if it meant not killing him, but he certainly had some way of having me killed before I got to trial. I've seen the movies; he would have some guy stab me with a fucking toothbrush in gen pop. I learned a lot from movies. When you're stabbed with a toothbrush, they keep stabbing. One stab would be awful, but that repeated in-and-out thing—fuck, I didn't want that. After I was dead, he'd find Marion. Even if the police kept him in jail, he would share his work and they would send another Jerry. If I killed him now, they would probably send another, but at least Marion and I would have a chance. We'd have some time. Days, weeks, months, years? I didn't know, but more than the no-time we had now.

In benighted states that have the death penalty, anti–death penalty lawyers want anti–death penalty jurors, but you can't be on the jury in capital-offense cases unless you swear you're willing to hand down a death sentence in some circumstances. So the defense lawyers make up scenarios to make an anti-death juror admit they'd sentence someone to death in some situation. "What if you saw them raping your mother and killing your children while they had a detonator in their hands that would blow up the whole city, country, world, universe, and you knew all this to be fact, and saw all this yourself, and they were creepy-looking—then would you tumble to capital?" I've always said that I wouldn't vote for it even then. I guess now they'd just read this book and I could be on the jury, except for being a felony murderer, actual murderer, and a hippie with no Social Security number.

That's not true. Even if you read this whole book to me (isn't that punishment enough, as all my words come back to me in shades of mediocrity?), I still believe that society should be better collectively than we are as individuals. Once society has caught the mother-raping, child-killing Doctor Strangelove with acne scars, there's no longer a reason to kill him. He can now be stopped from doing it again, and he can be stopped humanely.

I was totally anti–death penalty, I was totally nonviolent, and I was going to kill Jerry.

CHAPTER 21

I was a walking fundamental-attribution error. Jerry was a bad guy. I was just in a bad situation. His actions were caused by character, mine were caused by situation. In my situation I had to kill Jerry. I can talk. I can act, sell a scene. I couldn't convince him that my RenFest blindfold was real, but he seemed to buy that the magic notebook was in Niagara Falls. We were going together on a honeymoon to hell. There was still the slimmest chance I could talk well enough to not kill him, though I had no ideas yet.

"We leave first thing in the morning."

"May I leave a note for Marion?"

"No."

There was a brand-new black Pontiac Trans Am with a red interior and the gold screaming chicken on the hood parked down the street from my house, a stupid needle-dick muscle car. That must be Jerry's car. I would be going to Niagara

Falls with a bad guy in a black Trans Am. I already couldn't get Springsteen singing *"Even Burt Reynolds in that black Trans Am / All gonna meet down at the Cadillac Ranch"* out of my head. That record had come out a couple weeks before and we played it at the rocking RenFest wrap party. Maybe I would grab Marion's *The River* cassette and take it with us. She had seen Bruce at the Guthrie in Minneapolis on the *Born to Run* tour when he was the future of rock and roll. As I write this, the Boss is the past of rock and roll. *The River* is a good two-record set to enjoy while contemplating murder. The Trans Am probably had a factory-installed AM/FM/cassette.

Jerry handcuffed me to my own bed the night before we left. I slept like a baby—crying in my own urine. Not actually true, that's just a joke Eddie Gorodetsky told me. There was no crying and Jerry had given me a fast-food cup to piss into during the night. I didn't try to escape. Dragging my bed through the house would wake him up, and if I took it apart and went out the window attached to part of the bed, and got away, he would still fuck and fuck up Marion. So I slept. The bed still smelled faintly like Marion. I was so glad we'd used that pillow to prop her ass up. I buried my nose in it. God is kind.

Jerry slept late. He let me sleep late. He came in and uncuffed me. When we were together, he was able to control me by looking at me. That would stop any thoughts of escaping. But it increased my thoughts of murder. Marion had left some blueberry fruit-on-the-bottom yogurt in the refrigerator and I mixed in some Grape Nuts for breakfast.

"Fuck that shit, we'll stop for a proper breakfast."

"How would I know that? I don't really understand how being kidnapped works. Should I pack?"

"Yeah, bring a couple changes of clothes, and a toothbrush and some deodorant. I don't want to smell you."

"How long?"

"It's a fifteen-hour drive and we're not going to sightsee. Two days."

The phrase "a couple" sometimes means "a few" and sometimes it means two. He didn't say I needed enough clothes to get back. Maybe he didn't care, he'd get the notebook and he didn't care what I smelled like getting back home or even how I'd get back. Or more likely he planned on getting the notebook and killing me. Was he going to kill me in Niagara Falls? That no-loose-ends thang? I wished I could ask him how he was going to kill me. I could use some pointers. I had no idea how to kill someone. It couldn't be a fight; he would just win. I didn't have a gun, and he probably did. I would be bringing nothing to a gunfight. I couldn't poison him; I had no access to his food; I didn't have access to poison. I couldn't push him off Niagara Falls, they have guardrails and he'd grab me as he fell.

I always thought the hard part of killing someone is moral, but it's not. That's the easy part. The hard part of killing Jerry seemed to be *killing Jerry*. And I had to get away with it. Kill Jerry and then get the death penalty in some bullshit state? At least I'd save Marion, but I wanted more. Would Jerry and I sleep in the same room? Could I stick an ice pick into his ear while he slept? I didn't have an ice pick and I'd be cuffed to the bed. I doubt he was going to let me drive the Trans Am, so I couldn't make sure my shoulder harness was on and get us T-boned on the passenger side. I had believed that the reason I didn't kill people, except for that felony murder, was because I didn't want to. It seemed now that it was also because I didn't know how to.

Blunt-force trauma. I had to find something in the hotel room to smash him in the head with. I couldn't have a fight. I hoped the hotel room didn't have a professional wrestling breakaway chair that would smash over his head and just make him mad. A lamp base? I would take a hotel lamp base and I would hit him with that. One and done. No, I would hit him as hard as I could, and then keep hitting him until his head was mush. I did not want him to get angry before he was dead. I would smash him once and knock him out and then I would keep smashing. There was no time for indecision. I had to decide to do it, and fucking do it. Half-killing him would be worse than not starting at all. I had read a little bit about improv. I had to commit. I had to be totally in the moment. I had to keep the scene going. "Yes, and . . ." Yes, and . . . keep fucking beating him until his head was stew.

We were in the car riding. Just sitting in that dipshit muscle car, I could feel my cock getting smaller.

No problem, I sure wasn't going to fuck Jerry to death. I didn't need my cock. Jerry was singing along with Bruce. He was already a fan of "The River." The Trans Am did have a factory AM/FM/cassette. If you ever meet me, don't be singing "The River," it brings back too many bad memories. You can sing "Sherry Darling"; there was this woman named Sherry that I knew in Jersey. She's a memory that even Jerry couldn't ruin.

"I knocked over a lamp before it hit the floor, I caught it / A salesman turned around, said, 'Boy, you break that thing you bought it.'" Jerry was singing along. The Boss, one of the only rock and roll stars to celebrate juggling. Hitting the lamp with the elbow and spinning around and catching it. I'd done that bit at Ringling Bros. and Barnum & Bailey Greatest Show on Earth Clown College. It was part of our dinner-party plate routine. We'd worked a couple vase and lamp catches into the early part of it. I'd watched Jerry Lewis in *The Patsy*, the scene they now call "The Singing Lesson." There isn't much good juggling in movies. W.C. Fields doing the Great McGonigle in *The Old Fashioned Way*, then a few things in Jackie Chan movies. I learned to hit the vase or lamp with my elbow so it did a half rotation and then I could catch the bottom, which was now the top, just as it touched the floor. At Clown College we used very breakable (and very cheap) vases, so I could catch and save them, and then during the plate throwing I would catch all the plates thrown by all the other clowns without breaking one, and then, for the blow-

off, in relief, I'd throw them all at the vases and everything would break. It was funny, for clowning.

I was riding along listening to Jerry sing Bruce and thinking about getting to the room, grabbing the lamp, and smashing his fucking head in. I was just sitting there in the black Trans AM, like Burt Reynolds, making sure I was psyched up enough to smash his fucking head in at the first opportunity. I was hypnotizing myself with hatred and trying to eliminate all empathy. Eliminate all humanity. Killing Jerry would be a juggling trick. Just a fucking juggling trick, goddamn it. Catch the lamp and fucking kill him.

We'd left at noon and Jerry was already singing "Hungry Heart" for the seventh time. Man, this cassette was a great idea to get me ready to fucking kill him. It was now almost midnight.

"Hey, are we gonna stop?"

"Yeah, I gotta stop for gas. You can piss and I'll get snacks."

"No, I mean for the night. Like in a motel or something?" . . . so I can smash your fucking *"Got a wife and kids in Baltimore, Jack"* head in.

"What the fuck is wrong with you? You feeling cuddly? We're not stopping, we'll get to Niagara before dawn, and we'll get the fucking notebook. And if it's not there, well, you'll tell me where it is quickly, I can promise you that."

Fuck fuck fuck fuck fuck. "Oh, it's there, and I give it to you, and you leave me alone, right? And Marion alone, right?"

"Sure."

I wasn't convinced.

"Fill the car with gas," he said. "I'll go inside and pay and get some jerky and Hostess shit. Maybe a beer. You got any cash?"

I got out to man the pump. "No, I don't have any cash. I mean, back at the house I got a ton, and in the trunk of my car, but not here, not in your car. You took my last twenty at the last gas stop. I got like four dollars."

He crawled around in the backseat and looked in the trunk while I finished pumping. "Fuck, I don't have any cash either. Finish pumping and get in the car."

I was already done, so I jumped in. I wasn't going to run, because he'd catch me, and if he didn't catch me, Marion.

"We'll be taking off quickly when I come out." He reached over, unlocked the glove compartment, and grabbed a gun. He was taking time out from killing me to rob a gas station with a gun.

Fuck, the gun had been right there the whole time, I could have shot him. I could have brought *his* gun to a one-sided gunfight. I might have been able to win that. Would he put it back in the glove box? Could I break the lock while he was driving and shoot him in the fucking face? Could I jam up the lock while he was in the gas station so I could pull out the gun and shoot him through his fucking hungry heart?

In the muscle-car glove box was something else that caught my eye. There was his notebook. Another cheap little five-and-ten notebook, like Dylan wrote

Blood on the Tracks in. He'd left the glove box open, but I didn't want him to catch me looking at it, so I turned away. I stared out the window. Not much to look at, with it being Ohio and no one else at the gas station. I didn't give much thought to the notebook, what with Jerry walking into the gas station with a gun. He wasn't even really robbing it. Somehow robbing it seemed less bad than what he was really going to do. He was such a bad guy he was just going to wave the gun around to get some fucking gas and jerky for the ride. "*I got some beer and the highway's free.*" Before he left the side of the car, he looked all around. There was only one guy working the counter, a small Asian man in a green windbreaker, about the age I am now. Jerry kept his head down as he walked in, with the gun in his hand inside his pocket. He was going to grab snacks, show the gun, and not pay for the gas or the snacks, just leave a terrified and angry workingman, who, if he'd been American, would listen to Bruce Springsteen. Or maybe not, what workingman wants music by a guy called the Boss? Jerry would get back in the car, and we'd head for Niagara Falls where it seemed very likely I'd be beaten to death for not knowing where a fucking notebook was from a robbery I was barely involved in. What if the Asian guy resisted? Would Jerry shoot him? Would this be my second felony murder? Maybe I'd found my niche.

I watched Jerry walk in and take a bunch of Hostess products from the impulse rack at the end of an aisle. He grabbed some beers and I guess jerky. I had pissed at the last stop, but I had to go again, I was so nervous. He wasn't grabbing stuff like he was shopping; I could see from the parking lot that he was grabbing stuff like a criminal, and to hold the stuff he pulled his other hand out of his pocket. You could tell he had a gun. The Asian guy was watching him from behind the counter and had to know Jerry had a gun. That poor bastard was already scared to death. I felt sorry for him, but helpless.

Jerry approached the counter and said something as his gun hand began to swing up. Before he got the gun level, the Asian guy's hand swung up with a shotgun and blasted Jerry in the face. Just like that. No warning. It was so fucking loud. I saw an explosion of blood where Jerry's head had been. Fuck. I was outside the store, behind insulated glass, yards away, in a car, and it was loud.

Bank error in my favor, right? It was night and the parking lot wasn't that bright even by the pumps. The men's room was only accessible from the outside. Jerry hadn't let me go into the shop to get my own snacks. I had stopped pumping gas before Jerry went in. The cashier hadn't ever seen me. He didn't even know I was there. He didn't know anyone was there. He had to think Jerry was alone. Everything was slow motion. I had thought all this before the hamburger stew formally known as Jerry had even hit the ground. I saw the proprietor reach for the phone.

I ripped off my shirt and quickly started wiping everything around me. My fingerprints weren't on file anywhere, but . . . I'd seen people do that in the movies. My bag was in the backseat. That's all I had. Nothing else of mine was in the car. I reached into the glove box and grabbed the notebook. It had to be a different notebook, or he would have known I was lying and killed me already. He surely wouldn't have taken me to Niagara Falls for our killy honeymoon.

I threw the notebook in my bag, grabbed my shirt, and got ready to run. As I slid out of the Trans Am, "Point Blank" by Springsteen was still playing on the factory AM/FM/cassette. That can't be true, it's a little too perfect, but that's what I remember. The store guy was on the phone, peering down at Jerry's body. He wasn't even looking toward the parking lot. I got out and ran. I just fucking ran. There was very little chance he saw me.

I had my bag with the notebook, and I ran.

CHAPTER 22

Jerry's head was blown off right near I-90. The exit sign didn't say *Sortie*, it said *Milan, OH*. I ran all the way to the highway before I slowed down. Should I stand on the ramp and try to hitchhike? Midnight? Big hippie guy? I wasn't going to get a ride quickly, if ever. Hitchhiking was illegal. If I was standing at the ramp when the police came to find out whose face had been blown off, I didn't want them to see me, a hippie guy, at midnight near the scene of the crime. I had no cash. I had my wallet, with my AmEx (gotten without a Social, based on my bank account) and my license. I wasn't destitute. I was cold, scared, and so relieved. I didn't have to kill Jerry; more importantly, I could still tell myself that I'd never be able to kill anyone. Murder, of the nonfelony kind, was still outside my morality. That self-lie was well in place. I wasn't even a double felony murderer. Someone had died in the commission of a crime, but it was the perpetrator who got snuffed, and my role, this time, was semi-innocent kidnapped hippie. Jerry was out of my life and out of his own life. I was in good shape, except for Marion. Oh fuck. Marion. C'mon, white guy, talk.

I took all my clothes out of my bag and put everything on at once. I was still cold. I went to a little fake patch of woods where I could hide and shiver among the trees and the litter blowing around. I needed to figure out what to do about Marion. I would think for a while there, and when I felt like the police were settled in doing their detective stuff, I'd walk over the highway to the McDonald's. I could see the golden arches. If they took credit cards, I'd have a fish burger and then I'd call Marion from a pay phone. I had an AT&T calling card number, so I wouldn't have to call collect. How was that going to go? What was I going to say? Would she offer to drive to Milan, Ohio and get me? Twelve hours from Hibbing? Nope. This wouldn't go well.

How's this? "Marion, would you marry me? I've taken forty-eight hours to make sure I had no doubts, and now I'm most of the way to our Niagara Falls honeymoon. Why don't you come and pick me up on the way? We'll get married here in Ohio tomorrow morning and go right to the honeymoon by the big water. We'll go on the *Maid of the Mist*." Would the marriage proposal misdirect from "Where the fuck have you been? Why the fuck is your car still here?"

How to explain AWOL from her life for two days. Remember, Tiny, you can talk. Remember, Lucy, you got a lot of explaining to do. How do I explain forty-eight hours? Teetotaling had tied my hands a little. She knew I hadn't been on a bender. Could she be sure of that? People go alcoholic all the time, right? Could I get drunk right now and tell her I'd decided to try hitting the sauce? Could I walk to a bar or liquor store on the other side of the highway, get drunk for the first time, and call her while shitfaced? Tell her I'd decided to try drinking after the festival and now I'd sworn off the sauce? Full alcoholic and back to sober in two days? Why the fuck was I in Ohio? Why would a fellow do anything for forty-eight hours that would land him in Ohio?

I loved her so much and I was sure she loved me. I would tell her the truth. I decided that in the woods. I would tell her the truth, right on the phone. I walked up to the gravel of the roadside and headed across the overpass to the Mickey D's. Yeah, this was Marion, the love of my life. It was about time she knew the whole truth. I would tell her I used to be Poe. I used to be a street juggler in Philly. I could tell her about Bee. How I became a bank robber. I'd get some jokes in there about James Brown and Whoppers. I would tell her I was a white guy who could talk. She'd understand that. I'd mumble over the words "felony murderer." I'd tell her about Jerry and the notebook and how I lied and was kidnapped. Now the happy ending is Jerry getting his head blowed off and me being the perfect man for her. Right now, in Ohio, is where happily-ever-after would start for us. "Wanna go to Niagara with me, Marion? They got a wax museum."

I'd tell her all the truth. I'd go over Marion Falls in the barrel of truth.

I had the whole script in my head by the time I got to Ronald's place. McDonald's was closed. No fish burger for me. Just as well, it's shitty food. There was a pay phone on the side of the building. There is no place more lonely than a pay phone on the side of a McDonald's in Ohio at one a.m. I picked up the phone and dialed the number of our house. This was back when I still knew phone numbers. I even knew my AT&T calling card number. The phone rang. It was going to ring a lot. She was a fucking librarian; she'd be deep asleep at this time on a weeknight. I was all ready to tell her the truth.

She answered in a sleepy voice, "Hello?"

"Marion."

"Oh, Tiny, are you all right? What the fuck happened? I was so worried. I was worried sick. What the fuck?"

I changed my mind. I would lie my ass off. I *had* to lie my ass off. I couldn't tell the truth. I can talk and I can lie.

"I'm okay. Are you okay?"

"No, I'm worried sick and freaked out. This has been the worst day of my life. Tiny? Where are you? Your car is here. There's blood on our pillow. The guest-room bed is slept in. Someone ate my blueberry fruit-on-the-bottom yogurt. What happened?"

"I'm in Ohio."

"What? How did you get there?"

"I was driven here by a friend."

"What kind of friend drives someone to Ohio?"

"He's not my friend anymore. For that reason, among others."

"What happened?"

"I slept in our bed. That's my blood, I had a nosebleed, you know I get those when I'm outside screaming for a whole weekend. A friend slept in the guest bedroom and I ate your yogurt. Sorry."

"What happened?"

"Well," getting ready to lie, "there's this friend I knew before I met you. A slimy bastard I went to high school with back in Massachusetts. A guy named Ronnie." I was at McDonald's, so "Ronnie" seemed right. "Anyway, Ronnie was getting married in Ohio. This was years ago. And he didn't trust his wife. Well, I guess he didn't trust his fianceé, they weren't quite married yet. She was a trophy wife, on the fast track to being a local newscaster in Ohio. Teeth, tits, and hair."

"What has that got to do with *you*?"

"He didn't trust her, but he trusted me. He had some money, a lot of cash. I don't know how he got it, but he definitely wasn't a street performer. He wanted to make sure that if his gold-digging talking head divorced him, he'd at least have some cash she couldn't get to. He needed it somewhere safe that wasn't in his name. So he asked me to get a safe deposit box for him in my name."

"It's called 'safe deposit box' mostly in England, over here it's more commonly called a 'safety deposit box.'"

"Really? I never knew that. I always wondered which was right."

"Well, they're both right and if you're ever writing it, stick a hyphen in."

"Why would I ever write about safety-deposit boxes?"

"You never know—get on with your story."

I kind of felt I was telling a little of the truth. My real problems were also related to a safety-deposit box, so there was some truth there. "Yeah, so many years ago, before I met you. Before I moved to Hibbing. Before Ronnie was married, I was hitchhiking around. I knew Ronnie lived in Ohio, so I stopped to visit, for a place to crash. We talked all night. He said he didn't trust his fianceé."

"That's weird."

"Yeah, really weird—I trust you, and you aren't even my fiancée."

"We can talk about that another time. Go on."

"He didn't trust her, so he gave me a big box of money and shit, and had me open an account at his bank and get a safety-deposit box for him. All under my name. That way if she divorced him, he'd have his bug-out bag of money that she couldn't get to."

"That's really shady."

"*Really* shady. But what the fuck did I care? At the time he was a friend, though that didn't last long. We lost touch over the years. I'm a totally different person since I met you." See? I was almost telling the truth. "I forgot all about Ronnie, and his sleazebag money in my safety-deposit box. I don't know how he tracked me down, but when I came back from the RenFest on Sunday night he was at our house. He looked awful. He was fucked up on drugs or something. He did that thing that drunks do, where he hugged me and said he loved me. I hate that. He said we had to talk. I said I needed to sleep and so did he, so we slept at the house, that's who slept in the guest bed—Ronnie. I got a nosebleed. The next morning he said he wanted to go out to breakfast and talk."

"If you were going out to breakfast, why did you eat my fruit-on-the-bottom blueberry yogurt? That's my Tuesday treat."

I can talk: "I ate that before bed. I was starving. I didn't eat much at the RenFest rock party. You know that yogurt stuff isn't good for you anyway, it's just pudding with more sugar and fruit at the bottom, and I felt I needed the treat more than you at that moment. Greater good."

"Why didn't you leave a note?"

"We were just going to breakfast. I thought I'd be back before you got home, but then he went into the men's room at the diner and came out really fucked up. I guess he did drugs in there. He was talking about hating all bitches and that cunt who was leaving him."

"You know I don't like those words outside of fucking."

"Right, I was quoting. So, he said she had left him and emptied out their bank account. She threw him out of the house, and everything was tied up in proceedings. He wanted that safe-deposit-box money. Wait, it's 'safety-deposit,' right? And we were going to drive to the bank right then. I had forgotten it was in Ohio. It was awful. He was high, so I insisted on driving his car. And he kept smoking. Smoking in a car with the windows up. It was awful. I smell like . . . cigarette smoke . . . I was trying for something clever, but nothing came."

"Wait, did you take my Bruce cassette?"

I thought I was better at lying than this. "Maybe Ronnie took it. We had one in his car, I thought it was his. Everyone has *The River*."

"I don't anymore. I also don't have blueberry fruit-on-the-bottom yogurt."

"Right. It's really just pudding. So, we drove his car to Ohio."

"And you didn't call? Didn't you know I'd be worried sick?"

"I tried once or twice but it was terrible. He was screaming the whole way, and I was kind of afraid to leave him alone. Like he'd take off in the car and leave me stranded. Which he finally did, just now, in Ohio. We got to the bank, and he gave me the key that he'd hidden. It was probably hidden in his prison wallet."

"What? Prison wallet?"

"That means up his ass—I was trying to be all tough-guy."

"Don't."

"Okay, sorry. So, he gave me the key and I went in and showed my ID and got the safety-deposit box. I took out the whole shoebox and brought it to him."

"Why didn't you just give him the money and call me?"

She had a point. "It wasn't that simple. He opened

the box in the car, and it was a shit-ton of cash. Big bills, like drug money, or thief money or something. Hundred-dollar bills and lots of them. And there were some drugs in there too, and then all these Polaroids of his wife. Really nasty stuff."

"Like we take?"

"Exactly, but not happy ones."

"The sexiest ones aren't happy."

"I know, but these were just creepy. I like creepy, but you know, I didn't like these. Turns out she's now a real newscaster and he wanted us to bring the pictures to the TV station and the newspaper to fuck her over. He wanted to spread her pictures all over."

"What an asshole. Are you that kind of asshole? Do I need to burn all our Polaroids before you hate me and bring them to the library board?"

"NO! I love those pictures. Like I said, these weren't happy ones. Ours are dirtier but loving in their way, even the ones with strangers. When his Polaroids of her and whoever came out of the shoebox, it got bad. It was so bad I was looking at naked pictures of his wife getting fucked and not enjoying it."

"That's really bad."

"I didn't want him to use those pictures against her. I didn't want that. Because if people start doing that a lot, then other people will stop taking Polaroids. I had to stop him for the greater good. I didn't want to be associated with him. There were also drugs in the safety-deposit box, and he took like all of them at once."

"Like old drugs? Like what?"

"I don't know, they didn't have labels or expiration dates on them."

"Unlike my yogurt." She was taking this pretty well. I think she was buying it, in her way. What a weird fucking librarian. I loved her even more because she was buying my lie. She wasn't a gullible person, but she loved me. And it was a good story.

"I didn't want to be associated with a criminal. I didn't want to end up a felony murderer or something." Throwing in some more truth.

"Why would you be a murderer?"

Oops. "I don't know, I just wanted to get away from him, but I also didn't want him using those pictures to hurt her and our culture of sexual trust. I tried to sober him up. I tried to bide time. I told him to just use the money. I didn't feel too bad about him not letting her get her hands on that. I had proof he had it before he married her because I was the one who put it in the safety-deposit box. He took over driving the car and we were heading to the TV station to leave off the pictures. I didn't know what to do. I couldn't throw them out the window because he could go back and pick them up, or someone could find them and recognize the teeth, tits, and hair. I didn't want her to have her career ruined."

"When was this?"

"Today. This evening. He was going to leave them off at the desk for her boss. He was smoking like a freak. I told him I had to piss. His cigarette lighter, a Zippo . . ." Fuck, people who are lying always give too many details. Fuck, I sucked. ". . . was between the seats. We stopped at a gas station with the restrooms outside and he went in to get jerky and beer." More truth. "The instant he walked away from the car, I grabbed the pictures and the lighter. I went to the men's room and lit them on fire. It's hard to light Polaroids on fire, but I did, and I flushed them down the toilet."

"My hero. Well, some teeth-tits-and-hair broadcaster's hero."

"He figured out what I'd done, and he went fucking nuts. He came at me and hit me. I ran into the gas station and told the guy to call the police. Ronnie threw some jerky at me, swore a lot, and took off."

"Jesus."

"The guy hung up on the police. I asked to use his phone to call you because the pay phone wasn't working there. He said no and told me to get the fuck out. I walked across the overpass to McDonald's and called you." I ended with the truth.

"He hit you? Are you okay?"

"Yeah, he hit me in the face a few times. I didn't like it but I'm fine."

"Did you put ice on it?"

"No, I'm already freezing my ass off."

"How are you going to get home?"

Oh boy, she believed me enough to want me to come home. I'm a white guy who can talk. This was the first time I had ever lied to her . . . except the lies I had to tell about what had happened to me, where I'd been, and who I was. I needed to tell this lie too—it wasn't even another lie, it was the same lie.

CHAPTER 23

Marion had believed me, but she didn't want to come get me in Milan, Ohio. Can't blame her. I had to get home on my own. I knew the bus station would take credit cards, yet first I had to get to the bus station. I called directory assistance for taxi companies, and called a few, but none of them took credit cards. This was a long time ago. There was only one limo service that took plastic. The limos were for proms, weddings, funerals, and serious stuff like that. They could get a guy to me with a stretch limo in ninety minutes, probably the owner's idiot son-in-law who he would wake up. It was nutty expensive, but I've exaggerated the price in my head over the years, so I don't remember the real number. It was worth it; I would be traveling to the bus station in style. The idiot son-in-law wore a suit and a hat, opened the door for me, and drove me to the Greyhound. There must have been a better plan, but I couldn't think of it then; I still haven't thought of it. I had no cash.

From one thirty to three a.m. outside a McDonald's in Ohio, waiting for a tired idiot in a hat, is a magic time. I was still cold. Not shivering, but the kind of cold that seeps in and stays. Romania cold. I was too cold to think but I was still curious. I reached into my bag and pulled out dead Jerry's notebook. It was a little spiral pad like the ones Bob Dylan used for the lyrics to *Blood on the Tracks*. I opened it up.

Years later I went to the Rock & Roll Hall of Fame in Cleveland. There was a fancy case with the lyrics to "No Future" by the Sex Pistols, which would become "God Save the Queen." They were written in Johnny Rotten's hand. *"Oh God save history / God save your mad parade."* The words Johnny Rotten would spit out with venom just a few years before I was freezing at the Ohio McDonald's. The song that had been in my head ever since Jerry paused *The River* to steal gas and jerky: *"No future / No future / No future for you."* Those dismal words that were somehow uplifting. Years later I read them in a carefully lit glass case in Cleveland, very neat cursive. Not neat for a person, but way too neat for Johnny Rotten.

As I sat freezing at the McDonald's, waiting for a sleepy asshole in a hat, singing to myself, *"No future for you,"* I opened the cheap little notebook, and I was struck by the handwriting. Jerry, a killer, the man who was going to kill me—his handwriting, was small, precise, and gentle. There was no emotion. It was the handwriting of a kind accountant.

I don't know what I expected. I guess I expected
"All work and no play make Jack a dull boy" over
and over. Or "FUCK KILL FUCK KILL," or at least
"No future for you." But it was none of that. It was
just the facts.

Starting about halfway through was all the information that I had never had about our heist. There
was Bee's name, his real name, his full name. And a
date under it. I guess the date when Jerry found him.
Then a list of five other people who I had never met—
the rest of the crew. Nicknames and then real names.
The names of all the girlfriends, wives, and children.
Descriptions, addresses, phone numbers. Jerry had di-
vided it carefully. There were a few blank pages left
after each name for additional information. In each
person's section there were the dollar amounts and
lists of jewelry and passports and insurance papers—
the stuff they got from the few boxes that they'd suc-
cessfully robbed, or I guess *we'd* successfully robbed.
Everything that was stolen and how it had been split
up. No names were crossed out. But after most of
names there was a clean efficient little "X." I guess it
was smaller than that, I shouldn't capitalize, it was an
"x." Then after the name of the guy I supposedly met
with came me—there was my dead name. I hadn't
seen the name "Poe Legette" in years and there it was
in clear cursive. It was underlined once.

On Poe's second page, there was Tracy's full
name, with an "x." There were my two would-be
comedy partners, "x," "x." Fuck me. There was the
dollar amount I was supposed to have gotten, my

share. Not worth it even if I had gotten it. He had written "pearls," "diamond earrings," and then "DK's notebook," and he'd carefully underlined "notebook" twice. Reading that, I was the most scared I'd been since the robbery. When Jerry wrote this, he was sure I had the notebook.

"Six foot seven. Dark short hair. Thirty pounds overweight. Blue eyes. Loud damaged voice. Street juggler. Knives. Blindfold. Funny." There was a list of other jugglers and street performers. Lots of dead ends he'd gone down. Lines from my street show: "I bothered to learn it, you're going to watch it," "Final trick not juggling trick," "Turn executioner's hood into change purse," "Apple eating," "Apple sputum," "Let's run over get good seats." And then it was laid out: "Mick 'Tiny' Jackson, Minnesota Renaissance Festival, Shakopee, Minnesota. Pick up Bee Thursday morning."

There I was. He'd found me, and then he took Bee with him to Minnesota to confirm. The next page was worse: "Marion Lane. Hibbing library. 48 Silver Street. 218-772-0852. Five foot one. Dark hair. Big tits." Terrifying. Marion had big tits all right, and that was her address, that was *our* address, but that wasn't her phone number, that wasn't *our* phone number. The area code was right, but it wasn't our number. And there was no "x" by either of our names. Did we win? Were we okay? Had he photocopied this notebook and sent it to someone? Had he called it in? Had he told DK he was off to get Tiny and Marion? Did anyone else have our information?

Back at the gas station, Ohio's finest would figure out who Jerry was from his fingerprints. He was certainly in the system. They would notify his next of kin and then DK would know he was dead. Someone would get the Trans Am, and someone would check it out to find any information that was there. I don't think they would find any trace of me in there, because I had wiped it down with a shirt like I'd seen on TV.

DK really wanted that fucking criminal notebook. Did he want it enough to send another Jerry on the mission to find me and fuck up Marion? Someone would be coming for us. If Jerry had shown his work, they would be coming soon. If he hadn't told anyone anything, they would be coming eventually. We had a year or a week.

I wasn't going to disappear again. I was happy as Tiny; I wasn't going to be anyone else. My secular cycle of reincarnation had been actualized. Tiny was my nirvana.

The best defense is a good offense. Let's go. No future for you, DK.

CHAPTER 24

What did I have going for me? I could talk, and I had Jerry's notebook. Those were the tools I had to take down a crime boss. The notebook wasn't just about our heist. The front half of the pad was other stuff. Jerry didn't start a new notebook for each new job. There were names and numbers. The inside cover of the notebook had four numbers with no name at the top. Every other one was labeled. The area codes were all Philly, except one, 609—that was Trenton and South Jersey, near Philly. The first three phone numbers were neatly crossed out. Were these DK's phone numbers as they changed? A guy like DK, whoever the fuck he was, would change his numbers often and Jerry wouldn't put in the boss's name.

Our phone number was wrong. That was weird. Our phone number wasn't 218-772-0852 like Jerry had written, it was 218-437-4173. I don't even think 772 was an exchange for Hibbing. It had to be in code. I had a whole bus ride from Ohio to Hibbing to work on it; I actually had rides on several different buses. I had to keep getting off the bus and transferring. I guess if the bus were going from where I was to where I wanted to go directly, it wouldn't be a bus, it would be a car. So I thought on buses and I thought in bus stations, but you got it right away, didn't you? You just glanced and it jumped right out at you. "Really? That simple?" If that's what you're saying, maybe you're saying it out loud as you read this book and I hope you're in public and you look like an idiot. It took me about an hour to crack it. To decode our number, I took Jerry's number and added seven to the first number after the area code, and then six to the next digit, and then five, four, three, two, and finally one. You figured that out right away? Just looking at it? Bullshit. Good for you. If he used the same code for all the numbers, I had the phone number in Philly that Jerry reported to. I had DK's phone number.

Now why was the safety-deposit notebook that I didn't have so valuable? It couldn't be time sensitive, or he wouldn't have been keeping it in a safety-deposit box. I watched as much jive-ass crime movies as the next guy, so I figured it's got to be numbers of Swiss bank accounts. Or Hong Kong bank accounts, or Freedonia bank accounts—someplace offshore and shady. I bet you, Mx. Smarty-Pants, you knew the instant the MacGuffin notebook from a criminal in a safety-deposit box turned up in my story that it had to be offshore bank accounts for laundering money. Good for you. DK thought I had the notebook, the key to all his ill-gotten gains. For a bad guy like DK, the code to all your money is worth fucking up a lot of jugglers for.

Okay, Dear Reader, you are starting to really piss me off: you figured out why the notebook was so valuable the first time you read the word "notebook," and you figured out the phone number code just by glancing at it—so you tell me, what was my best move now?

I sat on the Greyhound, with all the stops, for about eighteen hours. I couldn't get the limo driver to overcharge me on the card and give some back to me in cash. The cards went through his father-in-law's office, so no cash for me. I had been at the Greyhound station for four and a half hours, waiting for a series of buses that would take eighteen hours to get me home, and I didn't even have a dime for Life Savers.

In between bouts of sleeping on the buses, I made my plan. Alfred Hitchcock said you must always answer the audience's question, *Why don't they go to the police?* Well, I sure as hell have answered that question. I was a bank robber. I was a felony murderer. I'd also be ratting out Bee and everyone else in the crew, though I didn't give a fuck about that. The rat bastard took me out for a Whopper and ruined my life. I also didn't know what I could offer to the police. I had nothing more than the phone number of someone who I thought was a criminal.

I would get home, take a shower, get some sleep, and call the number. I was a white guy who could talk, I'd play it by ear. I'd vibe out DK and the situation in real time on the phone and see what popped into my head. I'd talk my way out of this problem and get back to my life with Marion.

Speaking of Marion, I called her several times during the trip. I could use my AT&T calling card, so I called her at the library and told her where I was and when I'd get to Hibbing. The Greyhound station was less than a mile from our house, but she'd be out of work by then, and she would pick me up. Good, I was exhausted.

I didn't sleep the last couple hours of the trip. I was too tired, I was too hungry, I was too miserable. I couldn't wait to see Marion, but I was in no mood to see Marion. I needed about five servings of blueberry yogurt with fruit on the bottom, a long hot shower, and twenty-four hours of sleep. I kept running my bullshit divorced-old-friend story over and over in my head. I had to keep Marion believing it.

Things started to look familiar: we were pulling into Hibbing. I was running the first things I was going to say to Marion. Tell her how happy I was to see her and what a weird few days it had been. That was true. It had been weird.

Our Greyhound got to the bus stop, though I didn't see Marion. I got off the bus and found a pay phone. I didn't have any change, so I was going to use my calling card for a ten-cent call.

Suddenly Marion touched my arm. All my problems went away.

She frowned and said, "We have to talk." All my problems came back.

CHAPTER 25

There was a trend in novels a few years back where to get meta, authors would do a whole chapter that was just recipes for how to cook some food that kind of related to the story.

Here's how you learn to juggle a five-club cascade. You start with a three-club cascade but with high, loose doubles. See all that space in there when they go that high? You're going to fill that space with two more clubs. When your doubles are consistent and relaxed, work on a three-high—increase the speed of your throws so that all three clubs are in the air, and nothing is in your hands for a couple beats. You can clap your empty hands quickly while all three are up. When they come down, do another three-high, starting with the left hand this time. That's assuming you're right-handed; if you're left-handed, fuck you, it doesn't really make a difference in juggling. Jugglers need to make both hands as close to equal as possible.

So now you're doing consecutive three-highs, alternating hands, with no spaces. You are conceptually juggling five. But conceptually means nothing, you're going to physically add two. There is little satisfaction from juggling gedankens. Work on holding all three clubs in your right hand and throwing the first one up perfectly. Just one club. Make that perfect, high, relaxed throw while holding two others in your mitt. Just practice that one throw. It's hard. Get that nice and clean, and most importantly, relaxed.

Now it's time to flash. If you're a man, put on an overcoat, pull your cock out, find a stranger, and open the coat. If you're a woman, take off your bra, put on a T-shirt, find me, lift up your shirt, and show me your breasts. On second thought, men too, if you have a penis, I'm a stranger, right? Flash that to me. I think showing me your primary or secondary sexual characteristics is a good idea.

Now that you've done that, it's time to do a five-club juggling flash. Find me, pull out your cock and/or show your tits to me while juggling five clubs. Wait, you can't juggle five clubs yet. Let's get back to that. You can now throw one club nice and clean with two others in your paw. You're going to throw all five clubs into a juggling pattern, all nice, relaxed, slow, loping loops of doubles, but thrown very fast. The slow and fast is the great feeling of five clubs. The spins are so slow, high, and easy, and the throws are so rapid. For a flash, they will all go up in the pattern and you will catch them all again in turn. Each club gets thrown once and caught once. It's hard but so satisfying. It feels so good when that last lone club comes down and nestles in your left hand with two of its siblings, right where it belongs. I don't mean you bring your hands together like someone a thousand years ago gathering apples in a skirt, I mean all nice, clean catches.

There's no better feeling in the world. That's certainly not true.

Now that you've shown me your good parts naked, and done a five-club flash, it's time to work on qualifying five clubs. That means at least ten throws. Once you can do that reliably, take another break, show me your sex parts again, and now you can juggle five clubs.

My mom died when I was forty-five. I'm a mama's boy, and there was a great deal of grief. There is still a great deal of grief. There is no such thing as closure. I don't know what it had to do with her dying, but I decided to learn to play bebop jazz on upright bass. It's a hard instrument and I didn't have a good sense of pitch, and it was too late to start. Who cares? I learned. I couldn't really support myself playing—few people can support themselves playing jazz, but I can play bebop bass.

I took lessons from a great bass player, Murray, who was also a fair beginner juggler. He asked if, after he gave me my bass lesson, I'd give him a juggling lesson. I said sure.

He helped me with my time, pitch, and fingering. He gave advice on musical ideas and how to listen to the other players (contrary to popular belief, jazz musicians are supposed to listen to each other). He told me how to be supportive and comp the other players: "You'll lay it down solid. Always let the rest of the band trust your solid time and let them hear the root of the chord, so they can build on your harmony. Use your walking to lead everyone all together to the next chord to build that harmony. Let all the soloists build on what you're laying down. Let them shine. You'll do that for most of the song."

Then his advice on soloing: "When it's your turn to solo, fuck everyone! Fuck them all. Fuck them. You've been laying it down. You let them build on *you*. Fuck everyone else in the band. Fuck the audience. This solo is just for you. Play what you feel. There are no wrong notes. While it's your solo, fuck everyone." Murray was a man who had done a lot of time in the background.

All through the lesson he kept hitting on the most important advice for a bebop jazz player: "Keep your weight on both feet. Settle in. Feel comfortable with your stance. Keep your posture straight. Don't round your back. Breathe evenly, calmly, deep breaths. Relax your shoulders, don't put them up around your ears, relax, let them fall. Trust the tempo. The beat will come. Don't rush it. Let it come to you. Feel it. If you're relaxed and focused, you'll be ready for the groove."

We finished the lesson, and it was time to work on his four-ball juggle. He pulled out his beanbags. He started his sloppy alternating four-ball column pattern. I watched him struggle and panic. I said, "Keep your weight on both feet. Settle in. Feel comfortable with your stance. Keep your posture straight. Don't round your back. Breathe evenly, calmly, deep breaths. Relax your shoulders, don't put them up around your ears, relax, let them fall. Trust gravity. The ball will come down. Don't rush to it. Let it come to you. Feel it. If you're relaxed and focused, you'll be ready for the groove."

Getting my life back from DK would be a five-club flash, and with the addition of this chapter, *Felony Juggler* is now longer than *The Great Gatsby*.

CHAPTER 26

I was sure Marion had figured out I was lying or had been threatened. But she hadn't. "If you ever disappear on me again, stay fucking gone. You could have left a note, you could have called. You could have brought the Polaroids of his wife back for me to see." She gave me that big, beautiful smile and kissed me, much too sexually for a Greyhound station. She held the back of my head, stopping me from pulling away until my nervousness of being in public was gone, and I was kissing her like we were getting ready to fuck. We *were* getting ready to fuck. Then she was satisfied I was home.

"And if you ever eat my blueberry fruit-on-the-bottom yogurt again, I'll rip off your ball sack when you least expect it."

"I am so goddamn hungry. Like crazy hungry. I've had no food since your blueberry fruit-on-the-bottom yogurt." That was a lie. I'd stopped at a diner with Jerry. But it was also a lie within the bigger lie. In the bigger lie I'd stopped at a diner with Ronnie. I was okay, except I was really fucking hungry.

"You'd rather eat than fuck me?"

I grabbed a handful of her hair and firmly pulled her face to mine. "Either way you mean that, right now—yes."

"This is the beginning of the end. What do you want?"

"Blueberry fruit-on-the-bottom yogurt."

"Nope, you will never have that again as long as you live."

"How about we go to Sammy's and get a large anchovy pizza and a full Italian grinder, and whatever you want for yourself?"

Later in my life, when I did fasts for health reasons, I knew that breaking a fast with a big greasy pizza was not the best idea, but I was still young and it didn't kill me. I had been practicing my lie on the whole bus ride, yet Marion didn't grill me. She ate her half meatball sub and was just glad to be with me.

My relationship with Marion was fractal. Every part of it was perfect. I enjoyed eating greasy pizza with her more than I enjoyed fucking anyone else. She was perfect on every level.

She was the best. I needed to get home, have a good fuck, a good sleep, and then figure out how to stop her from being raped and murdered.

CHAPTER 27

The eating, fucking, and sleeping were out of the way. I was home. It was time for the important stuff. I drove to the grocery store and bought four cases of blueberry fruit-on-the-bottom yogurt. I didn't eat any. I put all the containers of blueberry fruit-on-the-bottom yogurt in the refrigerator. I had to balance one on top of the ketchup bottle. I opened the Tupperware with leftover soup and submerged a container in the congealed soup. I mixed containers among the vegetables. It wasn't easy but I got all forty-eight of them into the refrigerator.

When that project was done, I sat down and pulled out Jerry's notebook. How could this save me? What could I do with DK's phone number? I needed a plan. Also in Jerry's notebook was the number of the guy who was supposed to have given me the notebook. The guy Bee assigned to meet me and give me my share right after the felony murder. Bee had trusted him not to stiff me, and he probably didn't. He probably showed up at the meeting spot Bee had given us with my share, but I didn't show up, I was off to Hibbing. So that guy kept my share, right? Why not? You don't have to be a criminal to do that, and he was a criminal. No reason for me to go back to Bee. Jerry had gotten everything out of him. I was sure of that. I looked at the name of my missed connection in Jerry's notebook. Leonard was his name. It said his real name was Buster Washington. His parents had named him Buster and his nickname was Leonard. Jerry was careful, so I figured that was right. Poe who was now called Tiny had to find Buster who was now called Leonard.

There was Leonard's number, I assume in the same secret code as ours. The argument against Leonard still having the notebook was that Jerry hadn't gotten it. But it didn't look like Jerry had even checked with Leonard. There was no "x" by his name. Bee probably didn't even know that I hadn't gotten my share. Bee would have told Jerry what he believed: that Leonard had given me the notebook with my haul, as planned. Jerry might have just believed that. He wouldn't even check with Leonard. Jerry would figure that a felony bank robber would show up to get his share. Who's going to rob a bank just because they felt awkward after a Whopper? So, an "x" for Tracy, "x" and "x" for my comedy partners, but no "x" for Leonard. Leonard had the fucking notebook, and he didn't know that it was worth Marion's life.

If Jerry hadn't gotten his head blowed off, we would have gone to Niagara. Jerry would not have gotten the notebook from me. He would have killed me, and then gone to Leonard and added that "x." Whoever took over for Jerry now was going to find me again, fuck up Marion and me, and then back-track to Leonard.

Not having that notebook had not been good for me. It was time to see what life would be like with the notebook. I had three clubs in my right hand and the first one had to be thrown slowly and perfectly, a nice, gentle double spin in the air. Shoulders down, breathe, trust gravity.

I had to go to Philly, talk to Leonard, and get the notebook. Fuck, this meant lying to Marion again. I sure hoped all that blueberry fruit-on-the-bottom yogurt would put her in a good mood. If I could suc-cessfully explain going to Ohio, I could sure as hell explain Philly. There must be a reason for me to want to be in Philly.

"Hey, Marion, I'm really jonesing for a Jim's cheesesteak."

"You know, Marion, I have an irresistible urge to see the Liberty Bell. How is that cracked old bastard doing?"

"Marion, I got a juggling job in Philly and the money is good. I think I'm going to take it. I'm not doing Texas this year and I have nothing booked until next August. I might as well take the job and keep us in fruit-on-the-bottom, right?" Was it believable that someone saw me at the RenFest in Minnesota and wanted to book me in Philly? Sure. I'm good. Would she believe someone would fly me to Philly? Sure. As a matter of fact, while I was there, I could go to Head House Square and make some money doing my old show if it wasn't too cold.

No! Cold is not the reason I wouldn't juggle at Head House. What the fuck was wrong with me? DK was still looking for me. This had to be a pretend show. Let's make it a week of pretend shows, so I'd have time to get a couple of clubs in the air and start the pattern.

In my old life, I had a couple juggling friends who worked corporate shows. Scotty was an ex–computer programmer who still looked like an ex–computer programmer but was now a juggler. Jugglers don't look that different from ex–computer programmers. He worked with Katrine who was a lesbian from Denmark. Lesbians from Denmark look like ex–computer programmers and by the associative principle like jugglers. They told me long ago they had done some juggling shows for Blue Cross of Greater Philadelphia. It was that jive kind of "motivational" stuff—an excuse to juggle and do jokes and be paid mucho do-re-mi by a big corporation. Years ago, Scotty was trying to go from performer to producer/agent and wanted to book me at that same show, but I wouldn't take the job. I saw myself as an "outlaw" and wanted to stay on the streets. I didn't see myself as a felony murderer, though I sure was an outlaw now. I knew it was possible for jugglers to work for Blue Cross. I would tell Marion that a big cheese at Blue Cross had asked me to do a week of shows for a corporate gathering in Philly.

I had a lot of money in cash. I always had cash. I could cop enough cash for my plane fare without Marion noticing, and then just act like I got a check from Blue Cross. She didn't have access to my bank accounts. I was getting very skilled at lying to her. Maybe it was time to get married, now that I was prepared to have successful affairs. It's almost a shame our relationship was open.

I wasn't sure she would buy that Blue Cross of Greater Philly would book just a week in advance. How about Scotty and Katrine had an engagement, or Katrine had sprained her ankle? Sprained ankle is a pretty fem injury for a lesbian, but who cares? They needed someone to fill in with a week's notice and they called me. Perfect. That would also explain me buying the plane ticket in cash and no check from Blue Cross if she ever looked at my statement, which she wouldn't. I was a scumbag lying genius. I was so wasted in a nonmonogamous relationship.

That afternoon, I visited Marion at the library, and when she wasn't rectifying the lower shelves, I photocopied every page of Jerry's notebook for safekeeping. All these years later, and I don't think I ever had Marion sit on a copy machine. Damn. Well, other stuff had come up.

Over supper, I told her I had a juggling job in Philly. I barely had to explain Katrine's sprained ankle. That's the thing about someone loving and trusting you: it takes all the challenge and fun out of lying.

CHAPTER 28

Philly is warm compared to Hibbing, but it was still too cold to do street shows. That's not why I wasn't doing street shows. The reason was that I'm not an idiot.

I checked into my hotel, took off my shoes, and lay on the bed. I started to punch Leonard's decoded number into the phone. The phone made a weird-ass sound. I hung up and started again. This time I dialed nine first.

"Hello?"

"Hey, Leonard."

"Who is this?"

"Have you seen Bee since the bank robbery?"

"What? Who is this?"

"I'm one of your partners. Have you seen Bee?"

"I don't know any Bee and I don't know anything about a bank robbery. You have the wrong number."

"Listen. There's no problem here. None. You

are in no danger. I'm not going to bust you or rob you. There's only one thing I want."

"I don't know any Bee and I don't know anything about a bank robbery."

"You were told never to get in touch with any of those guys again, right?"

"I don't know what you're talking about."

"Have you talked to anyone?"

"What? What's this about?"

"Listen, Leonard, cut the shit. You got away with it, you're clean. Totally clean. You're safe. There are no problems."

"I don't—"

"I know, you're doing a fine job denying, but just listen. I was involved in that bank robbery too. I was the only guy you were supposed to see after. You were supposed to show up and give me my cut."

"I was there, just a little late, and you weren't. You could have waited a half hour for your share. That's your problem, not mine. I don't owe you shit."

"Did you spend the money?"

"What money?"

"My money."

"You weren't there, so it comes back to me. That's mine. It's the statute of limitations."

"Um, 'statute of limitations' is a legal term, and there is no legal here. We are criminals."

"I'm not a criminal, not anymore. That money got me straight."

"So you're the one?"

"What?"

"You are the only criminal to ever say, 'I'll do this one job, get square, and go straight,' and then do just that. Congratulations."

"It's what I did, I don't know about the other guys."

"If you're just living off the cash, you'll get caught. Money from nowhere raises flags."

"I have a job. A real job, a straight job. The money from the bank just bought me out of some beefs. It got me even and a little taste more. I'm sober now and I work."

"You're a citizen now?"

"Yes. I've got a fucking degree. I used my money to go to school. I'm done with all that shit. I've got children."

"Okay. Have all the money. It's yours. I wish you the best."

"Damn right it's mine. You didn't show up."

"Correct. You also have my safety-deposit box full of stuff, right?"

"Not anymore."

Fuck fuck fuck fuck fuck fuck. "What happened to it?"

"None of it was worth jack shit. There were some pearls. I gave them away. All the rest was shit."

"I want it."

"You want *what*?"

"I don't want the money, or anything valuable, I just want what was in the box."

"It was just these raggedy-ass notebooks."

Notebooks—there were more than one. Fuck fuck

fuck fuck fuck. Oh baby, please. Please. "Do you still have the raggedy-ass notebooks?"

"Maybe."

"Good. I want them, and you'll never hear from me again. Never."

"Fuck you."

"Hey, I just want the notebooks. That's all. You didn't expect to have my share of the money, you got double what everyone else got. That was a bonus. You got your life straight. All I want is the notebooks."

"I don't fucking trust you."

"What's to trust? You give me the notebooks and we're done."

"What's in it for me?"

"This is not an approach situation. I've given you everything I'm going to give you; I gave you all my money. You want to think about what you're going to avoid by giving me the notebooks. First and most important, you get rid of all the guilt you have from fucking me over."

"I have no guilt. You're a fucking criminal. You're a scumbag, like I used to be."

"Okay, how about this? If you don't give them to me right now, you will give them to me eventually. I will start by being annoying like I am now, and I will continue to escalate until I get the notebooks. See?"

"Shut up."

"You have one way to get that to happen: give me the notebooks."

"Fuck you."

He hung up.

I had told him the truth. I was more honest with Leonard than I had been in my last conversation with Marion. I decided at that moment that I wanted to have an honest conversation with Marion.

I was lying on my hotel room bed. I took my time. I thought about exactly what I was going to say to Marion. I thought about what I wanted to say. I prepared myself and called our home number. Marion answered right away.

"Hello?"

"Hey, baby, I'm in Philly thinking about you, and my cock is so fucking hard . . ." Yup, it felt really good to be honest with her.

CHAPTER 29

While that first club was in the air, I had to prepare the next one. How many Buster "Leonard" Washingtons could there be in Philly? I had found out a lot from that first throw, that call with Leonard. It wasn't just a notebook, but notebooks. He had had the notebooks and still had them. I hadn't told him they were dangerous; he had no reason to destroy them. I learned he had gone to college. He was likely in Alcoholics Anonymous or Narcotics Anonymous. He had at least two children since the robbery under five years old. Even back then, before the Internet, that was enough information to find him.

I could just go to Alcoholics Anonymous meetings around his telephone exchange. One of my definitions of bad screenwriting is Alcoholics Anonymous scenes. That's not fair—you could name a bunch of great shows with Alcoholics Anonymous meetings. That's just my personal definition. Maybe your personal definition of bad writing is anything written by me. If that's the case, even though you're this far in, you should stop reading. It's sunk costs. I haven't written, or even thought of the ending yet, but you can bet your ass it won't be good enough to make the whole book worth it. Don't be sucked in by that feeling that since you started something you should finish it.

When I was a child, back before this whole book started—before I was living and juggling on the streets, before I was a felony murderer, when I was just learning to juggle—I played Little League baseball. I was on the A&W Root Beer team. I think our uniforms had brown and orange on them and a big A&W logo. We weren't a good team. The other teams said "A&W" stood for "Ass Wipes." I don't know how they accounted for the ampersand. Did they think it stood for "Ass and Wipes"? Isn't "asswipes" one word? Children can be so cruel and so imprecise in their insults. It seems they could have gotten more bang for the buck with "Assholes & Whores." But because of the patriarchy there were no girls on the team, so I guess it would have to be "Assholes & Whoremongers," yet those qualities had nothing to do with our inadequacies. I guess "Ass Wipes" was pretty good for us. Children can be so accurate.

My dad didn't like sports. Neither did my mom. They hadn't asked me to try out for the team. The Asswipes hadn't wanted me. I sure wasn't picked first. Way back then there weren't participation trophies, but there was kindness. They tried to let everyone play. I would stand out in right field and daydream about being somewhere else. I could talk, and I was annoying, but I couldn't even manage the chatter. I couldn't do a convincing "Hey, no batter, no batter, no batter." I never caught anything, and I would get up to bat and strike out. My teammates didn't like me or want me on the team. I annoyed the coach. My mom and dad came to every game and my dad sat in the stands and bragged, "See that kid way out there daydreaming, who doesn't care at all about the game? That's my boy."

I hated baseball. I was miserable. It was a waste of my time. I would rather be listening to music, writing, and juggling, all at the same time. My parents had a talk with me on the way home from another of my losing games. They told me that I didn't seem to be enjoying myself playing Little League. They told me I didn't really owe it to the team, and although they were happy to go to the games and see me not play, I shouldn't keep (not) playing baseball for them. I told them I didn't want to be a quitter.

They taught me the most important lesson you can learn in life: quit! Quit anything. If it's not going well, if you don't like it, quit. So you can start right now with not finishing this book. Just put it down. And you'll say, "Wow, I learned a very important life lesson from *Felony Juggler*."

"What was that?"

"To not finish *Felony Juggler*."

You're welcome. Now that I've lost those duty-bound pity-fuck readers, let's get back to the book.

Alcoholics Anonymous scenes in TV and movies are there because in those forms you must show, not tell. I hate that about movies and TV. I would always rather be told what's happening than be shown what's happening. Don't show me a picture, tell me a story. I want sixty thousand words instead of one second of video. A book can explain what any character is thinking if the narrator is omniscient. Even without omniscience we have the narrator's thoughts, no matter how unreliable (that's not exactly what happened with me and Bee at the Burger King). I can write about my Little League experience right in the middle of the story. If this were TV, why would the lead character—and I am the lead character, right? That's not overly presumptuous. Why would the lead character tell that story? To whom? Screenwriters put in an Alcoholics Anonymous scene and the lead character tells the story to the group. The fucking drunk says, "I was terrible in Little League, and I didn't feel I could quit, so I started drinking." "Hello, Poe." Applause.

It seems I could have found Leonard by going to Alcoholics Anonymous meetings near his telephone exchange in Philly and asking some interesting characters about him over coffee at the end of the meeting. That would be a good way to find Leonard in a TV show. It could lead to some business. I could make up some interesting people who would punch up this section of the story. I might be asked to share as a new member, and there might be some comedy, with trying to share but not being a real alcoholic. I'd have to make shit up. I could stand up and complain about not quitting Little League while others were talking about beating up people they loved and stealing their grandmother's jewelry. That would make it easier to adapt this into TV. Alcoholic Anonymous scenes are cheap to shoot. It's just a basement, folding chairs, people in a circle, and Styrofoam cups. But no one is going to adapt this for TV, and if they do, fuck them. No Alcoholics Anonymous scenes in this book, I'm going to just look up Buster Washington in the phone book.

Yup—there, next to his name, was the number I'd called, along with his address. Fuck Alcoholics Anonymous, Little League, and the assholes who have stopped reading this book.

CHAPTER 30

The address, Cherry Street, right near the art museum, was consistent with his having gotten his life together. Leonard had the notebook, and I knew where he lived. I could break in and find the notebook. Getting the notebook was the second club to get in the air. But even though I was a felony murderer, I knew nothing about B&E. I only know it was called "B&E" because of a Lou Reed song, and even then I had to ask someone.

I didn't know how to break-and-enter anywhere. I would have to talk Leonard out of the notebooks. Or maybe scam him. Either I had to be crafty, or I'd have to wear a black watch cap and catsuit, and jump onto a fire escape. I needed to get to Cherry Street, though I wasn't going to just knock on his door. I had to find a way to meet him casually. Wait. Oh no. Oh no. Damn damn damn damn.

There was an 800 number in the phone book

for Alcoholics Anonymous. I called the number and asked them the times and locations of meetings closest to Leonard's address. Damn, I'm going to write an Alcoholics Anonymous scene. Fuck me.

There was a church on the same block as Leonard's row house, and they had lots of meetings. In fact, they had one that evening. Leonard had said "straight job" and "good job." He was a civilian. Civilians work normal hours, so he most likely would go to his meetings in the evening. The timing worked out.

I arrived at the church basement on Cherry Street. I don't have to spend much time describing this. If you've ever seen a badly written drama, there's one of these scenes. A big room, folding chairs in a circle. I looked around to see if anyone looked the right age and vibe to know Bee. No one jumped out at me. Luckily, there are a lot of bad screenwriters, so I knew just what to expect. The woman in the center of the circle was one of those NPR types. She talked like a Terry Gross tote bag. She asked if there were any new members, and I raised my hand, but there was no pressure to speak. Good. I listened to a lot of stories about how alcohol had fucked up people's lives. It seemed like a good idea for these people to stop drinking. There was some God shit that was vague but still stupid. After the final prayer, I headed over to the coffee.

I was just doing what any person in a bad detective show would do. Trying to start a conversation.

There was an open and well-meaning guy, his head shaved, knocking on seventy, but in very good shape. I walked toward him, and he introduced himself first: "Hi, I'm Mark. Is this your first meeting?" Okay, time to detect, but first it was time for me to say my name. I didn't have a name ready. I wasn't Tiny, not in Philly, that was my Hibbing name, and I sure wasn't going to say Poe, that was my dead name. It was time to be somebody else.

"Nice to meet you, Mark, I'm . . . Perry." I was Perry, like Perry Mason, but I think I really meant Paul, he was the one who did the detective work on that show. "Yeah, this is my first meeting, just getting my bearings."

Okay, now what would I do to work Mark? I couldn't ask him about Leonard, that would be fishy. And I couldn't go there every night looking for someone who looks like a Leonard, who looks like he could be a friend of Bee's as well as a friend of Bill's. I couldn't say I was looking for an African American drunk. This wasn't going to work. Yup, this meeting scene was stupid.

I had the address, so I walked over and stood across the street from Leonard's door. I was waiting for him to come home or leave home, and I'd improvise from there. It was a nice house. I thought again about B&E, but I had no idea where to start. I didn't even have a black suit, but if I did I would wear it without a dance belt, so my dick would look good, not Tom Jones good, but good. I just stood there watching Leonard's door. I'd been standing there forever. I glanced at my watch and it had been thirteen minutes. This surveillance thing was bullshit. Fuck it. I went up and knocked on the door.

The door opened and there was a big scary guy. When I say big, I mean smaller than me, but not by much, and that's big. When I say scary, well, he was just scary. He was dressed to minimize the scary. He had on a nice shirt with the tie loosened. He was freshly home from work, his straight job. He was a scary civilian.

"What do you want?"

"Hi, I wanted to ask you a couple of questions."

"Who are you?"

"Listen, is there a place we could talk?"

He stared at me. Just stared. He tilted his head like he was an owl at a bar in Tokyo. "Wait, you're that street juggler from Head House. You're funny. I saw you when I'd go down there to see my old magician friend, Bee." I guess the hair and beard was less of a disguise than I thought. I nodded. There was a long pause. "Oh fuck, you're the asshole from the phone."

"Um."

"Fuck you, leave me alone."

I had to think fast. I had to be clever. "I really need those notebooks you have."

"Fuck you."

I had to think of a good lie. I needed to. "Yeah, I think the notebooks are Swiss bank account numbers for a really bad guy and he thinks I have them and he's trying to kill me because of it." Oops, that wasn't a lie.

"Shit. Wait." He closed the door and locked it before I had even thought of one lie. I had just told him the truth. Now he was going in to get a gun and kill me. I was so fucked. My life was over. I needed to run away. I ran as well as I lied. I just stood there frozen.

Fight, flight, or stand there and wait to die. I heard the door click and that was the end of my life. But it wasn't. He opened the door and in his hand was a brown paper bag, a small one, like he'd bought a pack of gum at a corner store and insisted on a bag.

"Here, now fuck off. If I ever see you again, I'll kill you." He handed me that bag, slammed the door, and locked it.

I peeked in the bag. Three notebooks. Blue. *Spiral Notebook, 19 cents. 5in. X 3in. 45 sheets, Dayton, Ohio.*

Getting the second club in the air had been easier than expected. I couldn't stand in the doorway; he might see me still standing there, interpret that as seeing me there again, and kill me. He had done the right thing, and I would do the right thing. I would never darken Leonard's doorstep again. I had the notebooks. I had the fucking notebooks. In my hand was what Marion and I were going to die for.

I walked over by the art museum and hailed a cab back to the hotel. I sat in the backseat, riding through the Philly night. We rode past the groovy *LOVE* sculpture. I opened the comically little bag and pulled out one of the three notebooks. I would have to figure out something clever to do with DK's overseas bank account numbers to save our lives. Give him the numbers in installments as long as we stayed healthy and unmolested? Take the money and use it for Marion and me to disappear forever? My mind was racing. I couldn't just give them back to DK—he could worry that I made copies in order to steal his money later. He might also think I'd killed Jerry and want to punish me for that. Criminals, at least the ones on TV, are very committed to punishment. What could I do with these numbers to happily live ever after?

I flipped the notebook open, about halfway. There were no numbers. There were no bank addresses. It was all words. It had to be some alphanumeric code.

Waking up in sheets still smelling of you
Where did you keep our coffee?

Let's see. Have you figured it out already, smarty-pants? Huh? "W" is 19, "A" is 1, "K" is 11, "I" is 9, "N" is 14, "G" is 7. So, that number was 191119147. Was that a bank account number? What was I looking for? Add them all together and it was 60. So "waking" was 191119147, or 60, or divide one by the other and it was 3185319.11667. Multiply them and it was 11467148820. Or maybe it was just the first letter that corresponded to a number and then we'd use "W," "U," "I," "S," "S," "O," "Y." Now, change those to numbers and you got 1921918182025. You're not even reading this, are you? You're going to skip the rest of this paragraph and just see what the answer is. But someone reading this book is bothering to check all the arithmetic, and God bless you, but please keep in mind there's a mistake in there on purpose because only God is perfect.

This is where you skip to. It's not a numeric code. How do you get offshore bank account numbers to spell words? Even if you set up a program, and this was before that was easy to do, how does it come out as bad poetry? And this went on for pages and pages, and there weren't any odd letter combinations or nonsense words in there anywhere. I mean, it wasn't nonsense, it was just poetry. Not good poetry, but also not nonsense.

Does he put your hair behind your ears before he kisses your lips?

It looked like DK had written his own *Blood on the Tracks*, in the same kind of notebooks.

Oscar Wilde supposedly said, "All bad poetry is sincere." This was as sincere as a hard-on. Awful. Nothing but pain. Watson, the computer, looked over all of Bob Dylan's compositions and summed them up for an IBM commercial: "Time passes, love fades." They probably cherry-picked that summation for the ad. It doesn't just sum up Bob Dylan, it sums up all human experience. That's all we know, that's all we've learned. That and π. And we still don't live our lives as though time really passes and love really fades and that π goes on forever. If there were a god, love would last forever and π would be 3.

On the boardwalk, the cold coloring your cheeks
red
We fed seagulls and laughed while we shivered
My heart shivers and flies away like those loud
sad birds.

I'm not a violent man, but if this were my poetry,
I'd send Jerry out to kill anyone who saw it.

CHAPTER 31

I kept looking for a code. There had to be one. This doggerel could not exist unless it contained a billion dollars in offshore accounts, designs for cold fusion, and side effect–free cures for the cold, COVID, and AIDS.

I got back to the hotel and walked up to my room with my little bag of little notebooks of dog shit.

Here's the horror. There was no code. There really wasn't. The writing just sucked. Did he put it in a safety-deposit box because he never wanted anyone to see it? Nope—if you don't want anyone to see it, you burn it. He put it in a safety-deposit box to keep it safe to save it, it's right there in the name *safe*ty-deposit. Maybe he didn't write it. Maybe his daughter wrote it and then she was killed by rival bad guys, and he wanted to remember her. Nope, not a chance. This was written from a vanilla talentless cis white grown man to a traditional woman who he had probably called "bitch" more than once and beaten like Tina Turner when she sassed back. Let's do some shaving with Occam's razor here. The simplest explanation is that he had written this poetry. But it got worse. There were letters at the top of some pages. Letters like "C Am D G." The chord progression for every doo-wop song. I know it from doo-wop, but it's pretty much the chord progression for almost everything unless Steely Dan gets in there and adds numbers to the chords to fuck them up.

These were songs. DK had played these on guitar, maybe piano, since it was in the key of C. He'd have to modulate to B^b for his sax solo. I knew nothing about offshore accounts, but I had an intimate first-person familiarity with bad lyrics. I could have filled these notebooks three times over myself.

I was going to die for shitty poetry. I guess I'm supposed to have an epiphany here. I'm supposed to read this and realize that this gangster who paid someone to threaten the love of my life had paid to have me threatened and beaten; this dangerous, amoral scumbag had had his heart broken just like everyone. I'm supposed to realize we're all the same. Time passes, love fades. There was no epiphany. I knew we were all the same before reading his shitty poetry. I knew it before Jerry beat my face and threatened to rape the love of my life. I knew it before I was a felony murderer. I learned it in biker clubhouses and in jail way back at the start of this book. (Wait, I left out the jail part. Never mind.) We're all the fucking same. There's no god and there's no free will, but when all is said and done, there is love. "yes I said yes I will Yes." I didn't get all the way through *Ulysses*. Even with an annotated and explained version I couldn't do it, but I know the last line. I didn't need DK to send a guy to beat me up to understand love, and I sure didn't need his shitty poetry.

But here I was, in possession of DK's dog shit, probably with another hit man hunting me. I needed to be smart.

CHAPTER 32

"Hi, how are you? Is this the super-big bossman?"

"Who is this?"

"I'm the guy who has your notebooks that were stolen from your safety-deposit box at the bank. I also have a notebook from Jerry. Jerry, the guy whose head was blowed off by a shotgun. I have his notebook too. That's where I got this number."

"You fucking fuck."

"So, you *are* the boss? What do I call you?"

"You don't fucking call me anything."

"So, you don't want the notebooks, I guess I can keep them. I can just read, 'There's a hole in my heart and rain leaks into my soul.' I can just read that over and over to myself."

"Fuck you."

"Okay, let's just go with, 'You said goodbye, but I could never say it back, I never will say it back.' Just tell me, does it go to the A minor on the first 'back' or do you finish the line and then do the chord change?"

"Okay, so you have my notebooks. I want them. What do you want?"

"I want to meet you and give you your note-books."

"What do you want?"

"You'll find out."

"You fuck."

"You want to stop talking to me like that. You no longer have your notebooks and Jerry no longer has a face. I have the notebooks and a face."

"What do you want?"

"I want you to meet me. Just you and me. I guess I could say 'no police' but you probably want police around less than I do. If we meet, I will show up with two notebooks. If you're nice to me, you'll get the third, you'll get back all your notebooks. Maybe it's worth it to kill me as punishment and get only two of your notebooks. If you do that, the third will be gone forever, and I'll make sure it's the best one. At least I'll try to figure that out." I paused. "Do you know the only game one can win playing against an omniscient god? Do you?"

"What?"

"Chicken. I didn't just call you 'chicken,' or rather I didn't only call you that. The name of the game that you can win against God is the game of chicken, you chicken. If an omniscient god can look into hearts, He will know that His opponent is really not going to turn the wheel. And if He knows that, the opponent wins or at least ties. Chicken is a game you can always win or tie, if you can prove to your opponent that you are unable to change your mind. If you take all options away from your future self, you can't chicken out. You can't change. It's the way you safely listen to the Sirens. I will do that to myself with you. In chicken I must let you watch me rip the steering wheel off my car and throw it out the window. Then you know I'm not going to turn, because I can't turn. At that point there's nothing you can do to stop me from winning or at least tying at that game of chicken, you chicken. I'm doing that with these notebooks for our meeting. I will let you know with certainty that the last notebook will be destroyed if you hurt me. You can torture me, and I will not be able to change things. Once you hurt me, that notebook will be gone forever no matter how much more you torture me. Your only option, if you want all three of your notebooks, is to be nice to me. If you hurt me, you might as well kill me, because you'll never get your last, maybe best notebook after that no matter what. That's the deal I will make with my future self. I will win this game of chicken, chicken."

There was a long pause.

I continued, "I guess you don't understand. Chicken is a game where you drive cars at each other and the first one who turns for self-preservation is 'chicken.' You can also play it with cars driving over a cliff. You can play it with anything, I suppose. Is your problem trying to picture God driving a car? If it helps you, picture Him as God in the flesh, like Jesus. And if you want, you can picture that silly hippie white Jesus driving a needle-dick black Trans Am with a screaming chicken painted on the hood. And Jeez is driving that car right at my car. JC can see into my heart, so He knows I won't turn, but just for good measure, I rip the fucking steering wheel off its stem, show it to Him, and throw it out the window. This deity with a dick knows I'm not turning. I can't turn. I can't change my mind. The steering is out of my hands. Is that your problem? The visualization? Or is your problem how exactly I'm going to make sure your precious notebook is destroyed if I'm hurt. I can't explain my plan yet, but I'd be happy to brag about how clever I am—"

"Shut the fuck up."

"How about you look into my soul right now, motherfucker. How about you do that? You're already losing this game of chicken. And it's heartbreaking, because it's so easy for you to win. You don't have to drive some needle-dick Trans Am off a cliff, you simply have to be nice to me. That's all. Have you ever been nice to get what you want?"

"I want the notebooks. Where do you want to meet?"

"Listen. I'm going to give you all the notebooks. They are yours. It would be wrong to keep them because they belong to you. That's my motivation. I just want to make sure I can go on with my life after. That's all I want. If you get the notebooks, will you be happy? Can you walk away? If I can trust you to do that, we're done, you'll have your notebooks."

"I want the fucking notebooks."

"And I want to give them to you. I can meet with you tomorrow. I don't ask you to trust me, but I would like you to think hard about the game and what cards you've been dealt and what cards I have. I've told you how I'm going to play my cards. The only question is how you're going to play yours. I'm not going to rat you out. I'm a bank robber and a felony murderer. I've never been caught. I don't want to be caught. The . . . do you use the term 'pigs,' or is there some other colorful term you use nowadays for law enforcement? Is it now 'five oh'? Is 'pigs' too old-fashioned collegiate? Is it like I just said, 'You're the bees' knees'?"

"Okay, you don't want the police involved."

"Correct. And the notebooks aren't of value to me. I mean, I like good poems and lyrics, but . . . never mind. I hope you understand I didn't steal your notebooks. I was part of the . . . is the word 'heist' old-fashioned too? 'Job,' maybe? Never mind. I was just the front man. Part of my pay was supposed to be the contents of one random safety-deposit box and that happened to be yours. But I didn't show up to collect because I was too . . . chicken. Jerry thought I did collect. He thought I had your notebooks, so he came after me and got his face blown off. I wanted you to not send anyone else after me once Jerry was dead, so I did Jerry's job better than he had and I found your notebooks. Now I will give them to you, if you don't hurt me and don't send another Jerry to hurt me. I don't want anyone else to get their face blowed off, I don't want to be hurt, and I don't want my girlfriend raped. Did you tell Jerry to rape my girl-friend? Don't answer that, I don't want to know. I need to find a way to like you."

"Tomorrow at noon, bring me the notebooks."

"To your house? I guess it makes no difference. If you aren't nice to me, and don't make me feel secure, you'll forfeit one of your precious notebooks. I guess you're not worried about me blowing your face off. I mean that's one way for me to get my life back, but I'm not going to do it. I want to meet you alone."

"Fuck you, I'm not scared of you, but we're not meeting at my house."

"Chicken. Do you think of this as being nice to me? Remember, I can just destroy the notebooks right now, and if you keep hiring guys to keep finding me and get their faces blowed off, you'll never get them. I bet it gets more expensive every time to hire a guy to go get his face blowed off for doggerel notebooks. How about you just be kind and get your notebooks back?"

"Meet me at the Polish American Cultural Center in Port Richman. Be there at noon. There will be no one there except me. And don't call me chicken."

"That's all you heard? Okay, I'll be there." The third club was in the air.

CHAPTER 33

I walked up to the Polish American Cultural Center carrying a rented guitar in a rented guitar case. It was just a big stupid hall. If a miracle happens and this book is bought for a movie or TV show, they could use the same interior location for the Alcoholics Anonymous meeting and this Polish American Cultural Center final scene. Although now that I think about it, I bet the Alcoholics Anonymous scene would be cut from any adaptation. The Alcoholics Anonymous scene will most likely be cut from this book.

I knocked on the glass storefront door, stood in the cold, and waited. A guy came to the door. He was a stereotype. Really big square-headed guy. Not as big as me, but again, scary big. He was wearing a suit, in the phony bullshit respect way those fucking losers dress.

"Hello. I'm the guy with your boss's notebooks." He stood aside so I could walk in. At least the big boss wasn't sitting at a table eating galumpkis with his fingers and grease dripping down his fat face. He wasn't even there.

The gorilla spoke for the first time: "Stand right there." I did. He started feeling me up, patting me down all over. I liked his hand brushing my cock more than either one of us wanted me to. Sorry, I like people touching my cock. There was no weapon to find. He then opened my rented guitar case. He took the guitar out and looked in the sound hole; it was an acoustic. He opened the little compartment for picks and strings and stuff. He picked up the little notebooks that were in there and looked under them. There were a couple of picks that advertised the guitar-rental place. He put the notebooks and the guitar back in and closed up the case. He saw no weapon in there because no one had told him that, in the right hands, the machine inside that case could kill fascists.

The boss was making me wait. I'm not being fair to him—I was early, several minutes before our noon meeting time. The gorilla didn't pull out a chair for me, but I pulled a chair to the middle of the room where the guitar case was and sat down.

I looked at my watch. I no longer had the James Bond watch from my old Philly days. Now I had a Casio Databank. It was an early calculator watch that held phone numbers. This was the calculator watch that I wore when I performed at RenFests. I would not have fooled any time travelers. Other than my fancy watch, I was just a hippie. I was wearing a Dylan T-shirt, from his *Blood on the Tracks* days.

I had set my watch alarm for eleven fifty-five a.m.,

and it went off as I sat down. I hit the button to stop it and sat quietly for five minutes. The guy who let me in didn't seem chatty and there was nothing I wanted to say to him, nothing I wanted to know about him.

Right at noon, the big boss walked in from the back room. He was a different stereotype asshole. He wasn't a fat greasy fuck; he was a well-groomed fit fuck with one of those dark close-trimmed beards that I hate.

"Give me the notebooks."

"Sit down."

"You aren't giving orders."

"I'm sorry, I'm not. I was offering a suggestion. Just like when you said, 'Give me the notebooks.'"

He nodded to the gorilla, who brought over a chair, and the boss sat across from me. He looked me in the eye. "What do you want?"

"I want to give you the notebooks." I reached for the guitar case. Bossman twitched and looked over to the gorilla, who nodded. I also reassured him: "He already checked. This guitar case contains a guitar." I pulled out the instrument and held it in my lap. I didn't need a strap; I was sitting down. I reached around the neck of the guitar with my left arm and opened the little pick and string compartment, and pulled out the three notebooks. I held them in my left hand as I grabbed a pick with my right hand.

I sat up. I had the guitar on my lap in playing position, and a Rental Center pick in my right fingers. I reached out and offered the notebooks to the boss. There was no table between our chairs, making this gesture a little awkward. He reached over and took the notebooks, freezing for a moment when he first touched them. Our hands were close to touching. His hands were well-manicured and clean. My hands had tiny scars all over them from years of bullshit knife and axe juggling. I held my hand there, just looking at it, after he took his notebooks away.

He placed the notebooks in his lap. I put my left hand on the guitar neck in the configuration of a C major chord. As he opened the notebook, I started quietly strumming. This machine kills fascists. Third club in the air. I can't play guitar. I play bass. But I do know how to play an open C chord. I know a few chords in open position, and I can play basic barre chords. I'd learned all the chords I knew from a Dylan songbook my mom bought me. I had a guitar when I was a child. I can still play all those chords—not well, and I can't change smoothly from one to another, but I can get them to sound with my fingers in the right place.

He was shocked. "All three notebooks are here. You gave me all three."

"Yeah." I strummed softly. "Don't worry, I haven't fucked with them. I barely touched them. I thumbed through enough to see what they were. I was curious to see what Jerry died for, what you were willing to kill me for."

"What about your plan for holding a notebook back?"

"Yeah, I didn't even look enough to pick the best one. I realized I was talking out my ass. I couldn't

figure out a way to work out that chicken thing, because I am a chicken. I'm a coward, so I can't win
that game, even if you can't look into my heart. All
you'd have to do is hit me once, and I'd undo anything I had set up. Even threatening to hit me would
have cracked me, so why bother? Why make it hard
for you? Why make you hurt me, it's just making life
less pleasant for your highly paid sin-eater. Once I
got the notebooks, they were going to be yours. They
were yours. They *are* yours." I was still strumming the
machine.

"What's stopping me from killing you now?"

"Nothing at all. Certainly not compassion, grati-
tude, empathy, or human decency. I couldn't come up
with a plan to make you be nice to me. I don't have a
plan for that now. I would like to remind you that I'm
not the guy who stole your notebooks. I'm the guy
who found them and brought them back. Does that
make any difference to you at all?" I kept strumming.
"I thought about this meeting all last night, and all I
realized was I wanted to bring a guitar."

He looked down at the notebooks, smiling as he
read what he had written years ago. He should have
been wincing. He had no taste at all. No self-aware-
ness. That didn't matter. What mattered was he had
no shame. How can that be? How did a lack of shame
become a superpower? I knew that there were people, like real damaged or mutant people, who had no
shame. No empathy for the people they had killed
and the lives they had ruined—but it wasn't until seeing his face as he read his shitty lyrics that I knew

there were also people who had no shame for their lack of artistic skill and taste. He had none. And those are the same. The talentless dick was smiling. God bless him. Please, please, God, bless him.

I was still strumming as I spoke again: "Those are the same size and brand notebooks as Dylan used for *Blood on the Tracks*. Did you choose them for that reason?"

"Fuck Dylan."

This machine, *my* machine. "People who have seen Dylan's notebooks say that almost every line, virtually every word in each notebook, has been re-written multiple times. I used to believe that Bob got divorced and his pain just spilled out into pure art because he is a genius. Now I realize that 'genius' is bullshit. The whole idea of genius. Everything is just hard work. Everything is juggling. Now that you've finally got the notebooks back and you've got some perspective, and you've had some time, maybe you have ideas of what you'd like to change in those note-books. While Jerry was trying to find me, while Jerry was getting his head blown off, did you think about your compositions and what could make them bet-ter?" I was still strumming the machine.

"I'm not planning on making any changes. This is the exact record of my love."

"What happened to the woman you wrote these songs about?"

"Shut up."

"Are you going to show her what you wrote?"

"Shut up."

"Did you kill her?"

"Shut up."

"Are you going to kill me?"

"Shut up."

He was reading. He was holding them like they were the Dylan notebooks. I would shut up soon. I wanted to listen. I wanted to see how absent of shame he was. "Can you turn to one of the ones that has doo-wop changes—you know, C Am D G?"

"You don't fucking tell me what to do."

"Listen, goddamn it, I'm not telling you what to do. I'm talking to you about the love songs you wrote. Let me listen."

He started singing along with the machine. Fourth club in the air.

In my dreams you're still with me
In my dreams we still walk hand in hand
In my dreams your kisses are just meant to be
In my dreams I am still your man
Still your man
Still your man
In my dreams I'm still your man

He wasn't shy. He sang out. The chord changes were just where I expected them. Where anyone who ever heard a radio would expect them. The melody had the complexity of Lou Reed and Mike Love working together and compromising. Even with a range of less than a fifth, his voice was struggling and out of tune. He was awful, and I was listening.

And now, for the fifth club. I looked him right in the eye. The man who had ordered me killed and my girlfriend raped. The man who had ordered people I loved to be, at the very least, terrified and probably worse. That was just to me; he had certainly done more and worse to others. But he had done everything he did to me and the people I love for his art. For love.

No. What he did had to be different than other art and love. All bad poetry is sincere. But this was some sort of needle-dick self-aggrandizing narcissism. His love was different than mine. His loss was different. It had to be. His art was certainly different from Bob Dylan's.

And yet he sang as I looked him in the eye and strummed the machine. I listened and I watched. His eyes were moist. I had no plan. I had no hope. All the clubs were in the air. I had to catch them cleanly. They were coming down from their lazy double spins. I held his gaze. It was the same as playing bass. It was the same as juggling. I kept my shoulders relaxed and I looked into his fucked-up eyes full of the real pain of lost love. He'd probably killed her, yet his longing was the same. I could not find any fucking way to see his pain as any different from mine.

Mission accomplished: I was catching the clubs. I didn't anticipate this, but I had made my peace with death. Why would I want to live in a world where this motherfucker and I felt the same heartbreak? When we think of one-world, universal love, and everything we all share, we can't be thinking of him.

I no longer wondered what was going to happen. I didn't care. My fingers kept moving verse after verse of this garbage croaked out by a piece of shit. This was a fucking version of "Sad Eyed Lady of the Lowlands" played in hell. It was going on forever. There wasn't even a bridge.

He stopped singing and looked at me with a smile. "It sounds good, doesn't it?"

"No."

"To each his own."

"Have you ever said that before?"

He laughed. "Maybe not, but I believe you're entitled to your opinion." He was talking over my guitar.

"I am?"

I took a bad guitar solo that had as much integrity as his singing and lyrics. I moved into the final verse to end it. I hit the tonic. Then I put my hand over the strings, and we sat in silence.

The love in his face went away. "Do you expect me to thank you?"

"No, I expect you to kill me." I wasn't bluffing. I didn't fucking care. I had only one club left to catch.

I still had the machine on my lap. I started playing G D G G7 C Am G D G. Slow funereal tempo. I played the progression once through, and then I reached for the last club. I had no idea if I'd catch it. No idea if I even wanted to catch it. I sang, sadder than I've ever sung. Empty. Out of tune. I didn't even know the words. I felt such shame even in front of him. Good. He listened.

So hoist up the John B's sail
We have our mainsail set
Ask the captain something ashore
Let me go home, something please home
I wanna go home, something home
I feel so broke up
Please let me go home

Maybe Marion had saved my life again. I didn't know, but I hoped that she would get a chance to help me finish the flash. If anyone could do it, she could. Would she see the last club hit my palm?

Yes.

The End

Acknowledgments

Up until the Burger King scene where fictional Poe makes a different decision than real Penn did, this book is really just my early life. All that stuff happened. The only reason I changed anything was not to embarrass anyone but myself. I want to thank all the people who were there with me during that time: Mike, Marc, Anne, Beverly, and Tracy. Robbie and Teller were there too, but I'll get to them later. I want to thank my mom and dad—they are long gone, but they raised me so I would make a different decision about being a felon than Poe did.

I want to thank Bob Dylan for his fabricated first bio. He made up that he hitchhiked all over, slept rough, hopped trains, and worked carnivals. He inspired me to have my bootheels follow in his imaginary footsteps.

Thanks to Kari Coleman for letting me plagiarize her experiences as a psychic. She's also wicked funny and gave me some jokes for the book.

Thanks to Glenn Alai for being the boss of me

and the genius of himself. Laura Foley makes the stuff Glenn decides should happen, happen.

I always have Teller's voice in my head on everything I write. It's been fifty years for us—he was there then, he's there now. Love you.

Thanks to Steven Fisher for finding Johnny Temple and the solid senders at Akashic Books, who still haven't pissed me off or broken my heart. I may write more books just to work with them.

Robbie Libbon was there at the beginning too; he saw those street shows and now he makes my books presentable before Mr. Temple gets to see them. Unlike me, Robbie went to real college, not Clown College. And it's not just his book learning, he often knows what I'm trying to say before I do and helps me with it.

And to all the people who watched me juggle, listened to me scream, and then put money in my perfectly ordinary everyday black executioner's hood, thanks. Y'all kept me alive, kept me juggling, and I'm still screaming.